Direct Connection

Stories and a Novella

...ect Connection

Laura Farmer

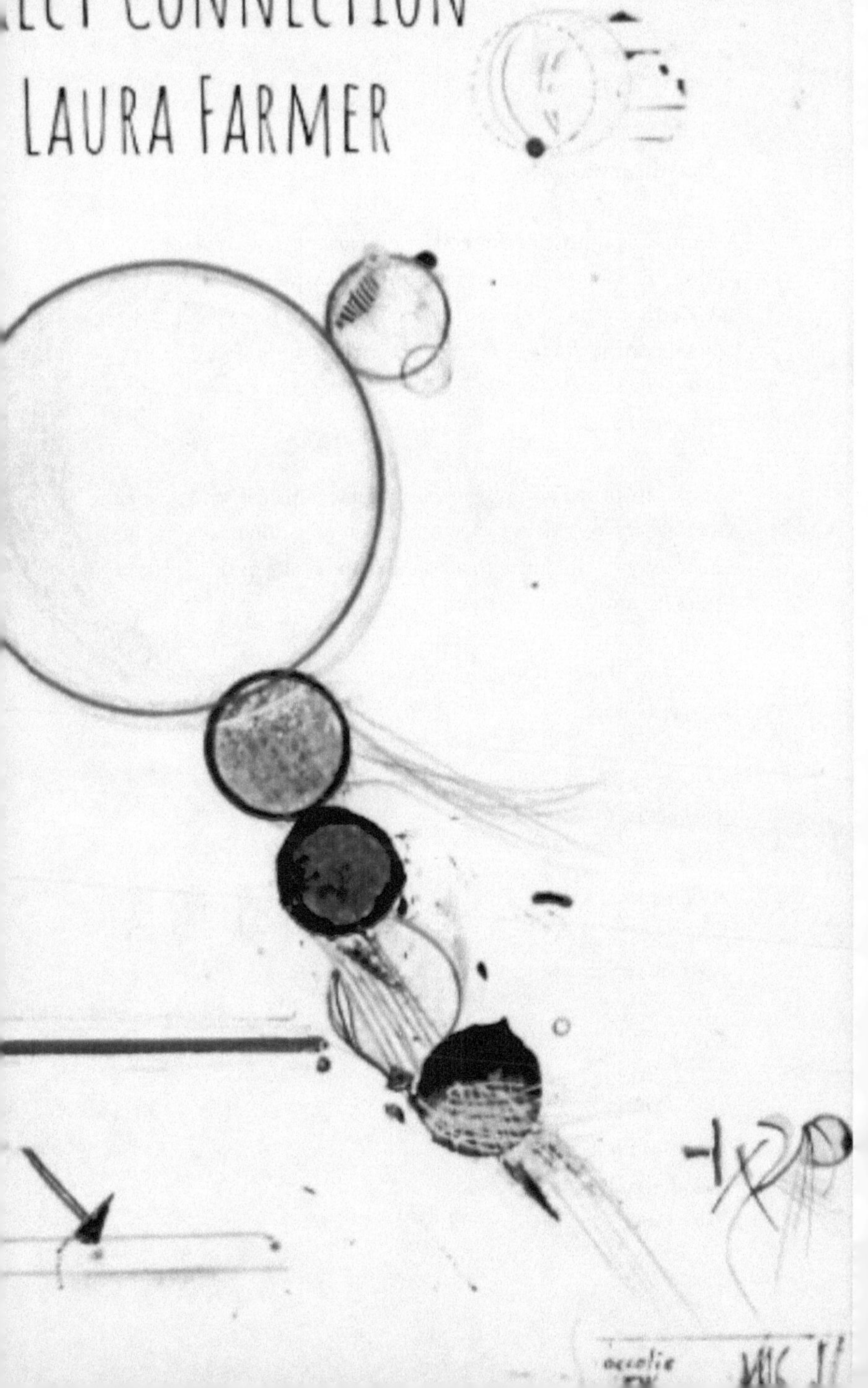

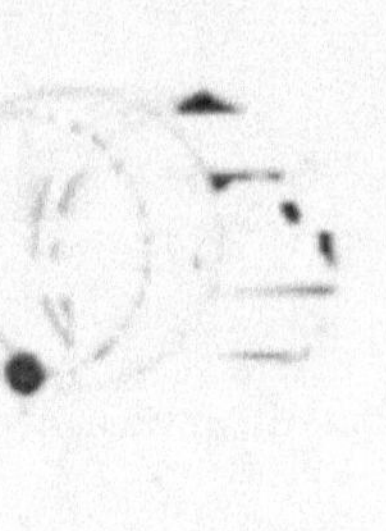

VIII

3

Stories

Direct Connection

Stories and a Novella

NOW

Beep Beep

The coffee maker.

The microwave.

The notification that yet another person, someone you haven't spoken to in over two years, likes the comment you made about your toast.

The toaster.

The alarm that's meant to get you up at six so you can go to the gym, but keeps beeping for thirty minutes, stopping and starting every five. Somehow you manage to always fall right back asleep for those few minutes, and that is when you dream the most. Yesterday it was about traveling along a gravel road with two very overweight women. You pulled over to admire some ditch lilies, and one of the ladies bent straight over, like that wooden cutout in your neighbor's flower bed. In the dream, you thought: *here it is, in real life.*

The security gate at Hy-Vee every time you walk out. No matter what you buy, or what you're wearing, you are always stopped by some very old man who has trouble walking over to you. You don't make it any easier. You stay right where you are.

A voicemail notice, from your sister. She says, in part: Heeey. So I know you really want me to come visit, and I do too! I really do. I really want to come out and see your place, it's just really far and maybe you could come back here for a few weeks? It'd be so fun to see you!

A low battery warning from your phone. You set it on the dining room table, and walk away.

The house alarm when you walk through the back door. You sit out on the deck and put your feet up on the table. Look at the yard you've filled with flower beds: Daylilies, coneflower, delphinium, winding nasturtiums that are just starting to climb all over. An outdoor space like this would cost how much in Chicago, you think. How much would your sister pay for this, and parking?

But there's nothing to do here, you hear her say.

That's the point, you say hypothetically back in return. You are five hours from her, in a beautiful location—a non-touristy beautiful location—so you may well have disappeared.

Someone locking their car with a key fob. You don't know your neighbors. You know enough to recognize them, enough to know which cars are familiar driving down this dead-end street.

Your watch reminding you to move, so you do: down the street towards town, past the bars and the coffee shops, and the dogs parked patiently outside, waiting for their owners. Past the catalpa tree, Denny's Automotive, the Casey's gas station with bikes in a pile outside, like the kids rode them right up to the door, right until the last possible moment, before leaping off and running inside.

Your watch reminding you to start practicing, that now is the beginning of your first four-hour session of the day. That now is the time you dreamed of before moving all this way. Four hours in the morning, a break for lunch, maybe a walk, and then at least four more hours in the afternoon.

What you needed was time and space, you'd said. That was what was holding you back from your greatness. If only you weren't held to a schedule, to traveling forty-five minutes to a practice space, to working extra hours to afford the practice space, to juggling practice with teaching and lessons and all the bothers of the city. (You'd stand on a corner, waiting with a pack of humanity for a delayed bus, thinking: there it goes, my practice time for today.)

The sound of the crosswalk alerting you to cross. You keep walking, farther from home.

Is this home? You think of home as a place you stay for a number of years. Not necessarily the same street address, but the same city. Chicago could be home, for example, but the apartment could change, did change, with rent and lesson income and saving, saving, saving, for a big move towards freedom. It would really be something to call Iowa home. It seemed too soon. And you didn't want to rush into anything.

It had been three months, about the length of your longest adult relationship, about the time things spin and turn and get a touch more serious. This was when Usman wanted to take you to meet the family. When Davi started to get tired of only seeing you on Fridays and maybe Tuesdays. When you started to realize (as you always realized, then conveniently stuffed away, then were forced to remember again) that in order for relationships to work, you had to give up at least a smidge of control. But the thought of that, even now, was still gut-pounding, like standing on top of a roof, or getting too close to a raccoon. You read it as danger, a situation to be avoided. So you changed course, got down, slowly backed away.

In some people, this tendency was understood, appreciated. But in others—in you, it seemed—it was a problem. It wasn't natural, you were told by strangers, friends even, to spend so much time alone. There was something wrong with you. One day you would change.

You decide to go full in. To spend as much time alone as possible. *So far*, you thought, *so good*.

A truck backing up.

Your security alarm when you open the back door.

When you walk into the living room, the piano is the first thing you see. A Steinway K52 from 1904 that you managed to move out of Chicago, across the Mississippi, and into this room. Before purchasing this little house, the piano was the greatest investment of your life.

You treat it as such, placing it against the main wall, in a place of honor. Where most people would put a sofa and a painting, you have a stunning, untouched, upright piano.

Sitting on top is an antique metronome, the same one your first piano teacher used, a fascinating, dated, overly-complicated piece.

Lu was her name, your teacher. She lived two floors up in a one-bedroom apartment. As a kid when it was time for your lesson you would race up the stairs two at a time. She'd hear you coming— barreling like an elephant, she'd say—and would leave her door wide open.

Lu wasn't from Chicago. She was from Maine—a place as far away and exotic as the moon. You'd live around the country and travel the world but you'd never meet another person from Maine.

Your apartments were very different. The place you called home was cluttered. Perhaps, by modern standards, a bit of a hoard. Stuffed with books, books, books on every available surface. Faded newspapers crinkling in the sun. Stacks of things your mother meant to get to, mail your father meant to read and sort once he found time. A small space in a crowded city made even smaller by stuff. You hated it.

There was no room for a piano, your parents said. How could they possibly fit a piano into that apartment?

Lu's living room had a piano—a Yamaha completely free of dust and clutter. Plus a small sofa, a plush chair, and a side table. And a gloriously large blue rug in the center of the living room with not a single other thing on it. Sometimes, when Lu would sit at the piano and demonstrate a piece, you'd lay on the rug to listen. You'd close your eyes, stretch out your arms, and take up as much space as possible.

The carpet was clean. Nothing ever stuck to you.

This is what it's come to, you think. Engaging in long flights of memory and calling it practice. Research. Inspiration.

—

The door alarm.

When you sit in the garden—first once a week, now a few

times every day—you think about how much better your life would be if you gave up the piano for good, instead of playing just enough to pretend to still be serious.

All the time you'd have to do other things. How much healthier you'd be if you could just sit here and enjoy the moment instead of berating yourself for not practicing. You'd have nothing to feel guilty about. You'd be free.

But I would miss it, you think. It's part of me. I couldn't not play. I couldn't not have access to a piano.

Okay then, you think. Let's get practicing. Let's get to it.

The door alarm.

This is the spin, every day. Down, up, up, and back.

At the bench you think about your classmates, their poise, their grace. All their success.

How foolish it is to be an adult with a hopeless ambition. The same hopeless ambition that was prized, praised, just a few years before.

It's been years. What have you been doing?

The coffee pot.

The washing machine.

The cable box.

When you stopped filling your days with arpeggios and Cho-
pin and other old dead friends, other sounds took over, like
digging a hole on the beach and having it fill in with water.

A different sound designed to keep you moving, occupied.
Falsely busy. Away.

Beep.

Beep.

—

You'd have other teachers. Once you started winning com-
petitions, your parents moved you to academic professors,
professional instructors. You went to summer institutes and
saw the inside of some of the world's greatest practice rooms.
Then came the academies. The fellowships abroad. The concerts and the prizes.

Lu followed your progress, sending you cards. At one point—
maybe after graduation? Or when you won the X prize?—she
mailed you her old metronome with a thoughtful note.

Looking at it reminded you of what it felt like to be in her apartment. What it felt like when playing was still play.

The feeling never lasted. But it never left you completely, either.

—

The sound of the mail carrier registering a package.

Lu died two months ago. Your mother told you the same way she told you about what she'd bought at the store that day, what shoes she decided to wear.

"Oh, and that old piano teacher of yours died. The one who lived upstairs when we lived on Beech Street, you remember? Lu was her name."

She didn't know any details, your mother. But she'd run into another old neighbor, and that's how she'd found out.

You wanted to ask about Lu's things. If you could go to the funeral, if you could talk with a family member, if you could visit her apartment for one last time. But by the time your mother heard the news, Lu had been dead for over a month. A distant relative had come from Maine, her things had been dispersed, and now someone else was living in that apartment, someone who never knew Lu, who would never know anything about her.

The notification that your oven is preheated. You open the door and put the brownies in. Mixes were on sale for a dollar, and you thought—*what the hell*. Twenty-four minutes.

No one talks to you in Iowa, and that's one of the reasons why you moved here. There's so much space here. Your neighbors are far away, and no one has said a word to you.

They don't ask why you are living out here, about why you left Chicago, any of it. You don't tell anyone about the X Music Festival, where you played Brahms like falling down a set of stairs. About the fear that seized your hands backstage at the Paramount, the sweating.

You don't talk about sitting at the piano for hours, your head against the keys, making bargains. Watching the life, the only self you knew, slip away.

A car horn, cheerful.

A silver, four-door sedan with Minnesota plates pulls into your driveway. You don't drive, and you didn't order anything. For some reason your first thought is that the car is a rental.

You watch a grown woman—an elderly woman, really— unload a bag and a small cooler.

Then she goes around to the trunk and starts yelling for you.

You realize then that you've been standing at the window, watching like this wasn't your real life.

Is this your real life?

"Grab that bag out of the trunk, will you?" she says.

Lu is a rounder version of herself. Still short, with her thick glasses, but now with a swollen stomach that looks more like a medical condition than fat: firm and round, like something you could drain. Her face hasn't aged, you think. She laughs just like you remembered.

You look up at the sky. Feel the wind on your face. Can you feel wind in a dream, you wonder? Can you feel how heavy a bag is?

Something in her bag.

She tells you to get in there and make it stop.

This is the moment you give in.

"Just root around in there," she says. "There's nothing sharp."

Lu is the first person to visit you. And even if she's not real, she's still the first person to come visit you. And seeing her standing there you feel a wave of assurance, of complete understanding.

You worry for a moment that you'll wet yourself. That you'll lose it completely right there in the driveway.

She takes her shoes off, puts her bag on the floor. She rubs her hand affectionally on the back of the sofa. She looks around the room, then at you, and smiles. She's happy for you, proud of you. Even though.

She looks at you and nods.

"Okay," she says. "Show me."

You do as you always did with her. You leave the room to clear the air. Then walk back in and stand next to the piano for five seconds, imagining the audience, their polite applause of welcome. Then you sit, and begin.

You're embarrassed that the piano is dusty. You push back the lid and the keys are clean, gleaming, waiting. You stare at them.

You haven't played in six months. More. You keep staring.

The timer on the oven.

You keep staring at the piano. You think maybe Lu won't notice that you aren't playing. That maybe she thinks the timer is drowning you out. That if only that darn timer would stop, then she could hear you.

The timer on the oven.

Maybe you were never really very good at the piano. Maybe there was a time limit, an expiration date to talent.

The timer on the oven.

Lu hefts herself up and goes into the kitchen.

She gets right in there, finds the oven mitts, takes the brownies out, and comes back. She doesn't look at you directly, because she knows you would break.

"I'm not as small as I used to be," she says, crowding next to you on the bench. She's warm and soft, and sitting that close to her feels like passing through a cloud.

———

Your alarm.

Your alarm.

You walk down the hall in your bare feet. And there she is, sleeping on your sofa.

Still here.

You go back into your bedroom and close the door.

You are ready for this, you think. But not yet. You go back to bed.

—

The alert that the door is ajar.

Lu packs a picnic and you set off to explore town. She knew you hadn't been out beyond the gas station, that you would have felt too guilty taking a hike or walking through the taxidermy shop or even chatting with anyone because you should have been practicing. All that time, you should have been practicing.

But with a guest, things are different.

You go to a forest just three blocks away and hike. At the top of a hill you have bagels, fresh iced tea, pineapple. Brownies. Just food you had at the house. But now, here, everything is delicious. Special.

You spread out a blanket and lay on it together. Taking up as much space as possible.

The sky is enormous.

"Let's just close our eyes a minute," she says. Like the park, everything, is yours.

You hear nothing. Only blankness. The same blankness that has followed you for months. And then.

The call of a chickadee.

The wind through a maple tree.

The gentle shuffle of someone on the trail.

Other sounds, other sounds.

"Just listen," she says.

—

The next day you walk to a construction site and watch a wheezy multi-family house get demolished. Lu brought a blanket and a thermos of coffee. This is your morning.

When the back half falls away you can see inside—the pink, flowered wallpaper; the water-damaged ceilings. You and Lu make up stories about who lived in each room, what they ate for breakfast. Who they loved, what their voices sounded like.

The rattle of a chain.

The pregnant silence of the excavator reaching above the back bedroom, then crashing through the roof.

The crunch of the roof as it gives way.

It's an orchestra of sorts, you think, scaring yourself. A song. You can hear it.

—

In the middle of the night, Lu gets you out of bed.

The windows in the living room are wide open, and the whole room is filled with that wet, summer air that smells like the forest, a smell so different from everything you knew in the city that even now, after all this time, it still makes you feel a bit panicked. Like you got lost.

Sitting on the piano bench together, your hair greasy, your mouth sticky, she explains that all your neighbors are asleep. The adults, the children, their pets. Every one of them.

"They have soundtracks," she says. "That's how their dreams move. Listen."

And you do. You sit on the bench, unafraid.

The steady rhythm of the cricket.

The hum of the streetlight.

The jingle of a dog's leash.

—

On her last day, Lu asks you to come help her with something.

She's leaning against the piano.

"I have an idea," she says.

Your one-bedroom house is laid out in a grid: living and din-ing room in front, kitchen and bedroom in the back, with one small bathroom in-between.

The piano is in the living room, against the main wall, so when you play—hypothetically—your back is to the picture window.

So when you walk in the house, the piano is the first thing you see.

So when you lay on the couch, the only cozy spot other than your bed, you look right at the piano. At what you should be doing. At what you always should be doing.

The doorbell.

The doorbell.

"Go on," she says. "Answer it."

She'd called the moving company, the same one that moved you in. The one that kept a piano tuner on retainer.

"You'd be surprised how many people move up here with a piano," the man had told you.

Now here they were again. No nonsense, no questions.

They move the piano into the dining room, then move the table and chairs against the far wall.

You return to the living room, now a wide-open space. You have them put the sofa where the piano had been, so when you lay on it, you look out the big window, up at the neighbor's pine trees.

Lu puts the extra chair in the corner. Extra seating, she says.

The center rug looks bigger than ever.

You never talked about why she was visiting, what she was doing just by being there. She moved furniture around with the gentle confidence of someone who had known you your entire life, who knew you better in that moment than you knew yourself. Who was there for you and who would never leave you even though you would never see her again.

The shush of sliding a table across the carpet.

The hum of a car passing.

Other sounds, other sounds.

—

Friday Lu was gone.

You sit on the sofa all morning, looking out the window. Listening.

In the afternoon, you walk. When you pass a neighbor out mowing, you raise your hand. He raises his in return.

That night, you sit at the piano. The dining room is cozy, warm.

You set your hands down on the keyboard.

Here you are, you think. Here I am.

And after some trial and error, you find the pitch exactly.

Once. Twice. A sound all your own.

Beep.

Beep.

Direct Connection

The first time I saw the telephone I was driving home from work.
The same route every day, then suddenly—something different.
I'm idling, listening to KZIA, window rolled down, and there it
was on the retaining wall across the street. At 7th and 31st. Right
by the American Legion.

It's not an exaggeration to say I've never seen a stencil tag in Cedar Rapids. There's loopy teenage scroll under the bridge by Ellis Park. One of those peeing Calvin cartoons on the wall behind the Blue Room Lounge. Small, unobtrusive things.

But a print like this was the sort of thing I'd see in Prague when we went on family trips. Beautiful, edgy stuff with meanings I couldn't master thanks to my rudimentary Czech.

It was big, at least four feet tall. The swagger of it made me proud. Iowans aren't known for swagger.

I said something to Regina, my neighbor, when I got home. She was bent over the rain barrel with a watering can, still in her nice call center clothes.

"These tomatoes are so dry!" she said. "I just had to get after them right away."

"You see that graffiti over by the Legion?" I said.

"No," she said, hefting the can up. "God, landlines. Remember those clear phones where you could see all the guts inside? I had one of those in my room in high school. Wonder whatever happened to that."

I couldn't stop thinking about that tag. But I wouldn't say anything to my coworkers at Zinc, a web design company in one of those shiny new factory overhauls downtown. Our building was stuffed with pool tables and communal work spaces and bars and fridges stocked full of free goodies. Just like a company store, but you paid with your time.

I wear jeans to work every day, but I iron my t-shirts. Wear a suit jacket. Old habits.

Mom worked at the Blue Room for years, standing behind the bar. She shined her shoes every night. "It's not for them," she'd say.

At Zinc, I spend most of my days trying to take up as much space as possible so people don't sit next to me. Every morning I get there early and unload all over a table: a coffee mug, a glass of water, two pencils, three pens, a sketchpad, some drawings, some receipts, some spreadsheets. Some days, if I'm really feeling the space, I get out my charcoals and make the table all dusty.

Most of the guys at work call me Eddie. I like it, and I know what it means: that I'm on the same level as them. Calling me something masculine means I'm more like them than not. It's supposed to be a compliment.

If a guy's new, or pissed at me, he'll call me by my full name: Edita. To take me down a peg, remind me that I don't really belong.

Your own name gets used against you.

"Kill 'em with kindness," my mother used to say when I was a kid. My mother was a small woman, just over five feet. She died before smartphones, before the internet was really a thing.

The day after I saw the telephone I called in and took the day to drive around Cedar Rapids and who knows where else—Marion? Fairfax?—looking for more tags. I'd make a day of it, I decided, and got coffee and a roll from the Kettle House.

I hadn't taken a day off in months.

We—well, I—still have a landline at home, a cradle phone in an honest-to-God telephone nook that came with the place. Most people think it's just for show, but it works.

Growing up, my family had a wall mount in the kitchen, the heavy sort that acted more like an appliance than something personal. There wasn't much privacy as kids, but if it's all you know you don't notice it. There was just the one phone, right in the center of everything. And when Grandma would call from Texas and Dad would stand there vacant, silent, you just read in your bunk. Curled up behind the rocking chair with headphones and listened to Mom's weird European albums. Or traced your feet, over and over again, in chalk on the cellar floor. It was a small house, but there were always small places to burrow in and make your own.

I drive now, and new homes are bloated like ticks, the construction hurried and shoddy. My ex knows all these guys, the contractors, the electricians, the guys behind the pro desk at Home Depot.

"I'm glad we have an old house," she always said. "This ain't going nowhere."

Sue works as a painter. She runs a small crew of guys and has two trucks, a pile of brushes, rollers, extenders and ladders, and a number of yard signs. When they're on a job, she puts the sign in the client's yard, a small white square that says "The Paint Crew" with a phone number. It's a stencil, sprayed in black.

They don't have a website. The phone number is our house phone.

Sue started the crew before we met, and it's been going for seven years now. Just longer than we did. She makes surprisingly good money for six months of work, just picking up whatever jobs she wants. About $40,000 when all's said and done.

When we met Sue was renting a little apartment and the garage behind, where she stored all the equipment.

I asked what she did all winter. "Cross-country ski," she said. "Make a lot of chili. And there's Christmas."

Even when Sue was single she was big on Christmas. Beginning just before Thanksgiving she'd start a plan of volunteer efforts, decorating blitzes, and community work. She loved having the freedom, the flexibility.

"I could make more money," she said. "But who cares?"

—

I wouldn't always tell Sue when I took time off. I had the time, and it was my business. That was just our way. She was all over the area for work, so I didn't know where she was half the time either. Some nights she'd be home before me, cooking some sort of stew with beer in it, or I wouldn't see her until after eight, when she came in splattered in paint. We were in and out.

It was summer. I was thirty-two. Sue was thirty-six.

We had plans. This was how we worked it: I paid for the house in cash, a little two bedroom near the old train line. Sue paid the bills: the electric, the gas, the water. We only spent what she brought in. My salary went towards home repairs, flowers (because yeah), Christmas decorations (of course), and savings. Every winter we took a big trip, somewhere we could ski and do intense sled runs. Germany was a favorite spot, Finland. Last summer we ditched down to Argentina for two weeks and had one of the best times of our lives.

Moving this way, I thought, we could retire by forty-five. And still have plenty of fun.

Besides, Sue's great for travel. She's laid back, up for anything, and every man wants to be her friend. We'd always meet people, always find our way into someone's home.

"Let's not ski today," she'd say at least once on every trip. "Let's just see who's around." In Les Saisies Sue ended up spending two days at some guy's house helping him paint a ceiling. Sue barely spoke French, but there the two of them were, up on their backs on a scaffold, cracking each other up.

The man (Claude? Clément?) had a mother not far down the road, so I went to see her, helped with her shopping, walked around the town with her holding my hand.

I called those *Quantum Leap* moments—times where if my younger self were to suddenly jump into my body, she'd be so pleasantly dumbfounded. Especially to see Sue, leaning out a second story window, spotted in paint, blowing me a kiss.

—

I didn't see it coming, is what I would have told someone. If I told someone, which I didn't. I didn't tell anyone.

Sue had been seeing Tasha, my oldest friend, my friend I'd known since grade school, when we ran around on bikes together, getting cherry Freezes, swimming in the creek, laying on our backs at Sartori Park for hours, just watching the clouds, telling stories, smacking bugs.

Tasha, of all people.

"I don't know how to explain it," Sue said one night two weeks ago. Two weeks and one day ago. She just out and told me. "It's the craziest thing."

"But Tasha isn't into women," I said dumbly.

She wasn't leaving me for Tasha, she wanted to make that clear. She was just leaving.

Was that worse? It felt worse.

I worked overtime, stayed late and played pool, took on extra projects. I stuffed my days full.

Because it was all the things you notice: Sue's ratty old work boots were gone, the ones I'd slip my bare feet into when I needed to quick run down to the cellar. Her coffee mug, the stack of beer cozies. I didn't have to clean the mud room every night, run the vacuum every night. I'd come home from work and my loose change would be exactly where I'd left it.

I said she could have the house. It was paid for, I could buy something else.

"I think I'll get a camper, a little guy for the truck. I think I'm just going to travel around awhile. Maybe go out to the desert."

"Is Tasha going?"

She laughed and shook her head, like we were still together, or like we were friends. Like we knew each other at all. "Could you see Tasha in something like that?"

Where was I going again?

Turn left, turn right.

I'd met Sue at a bar when I was back in Iowa taking care of my mother, and before all that, before we met, before I stayed and we got moving, I'd been bouncing around, a different city every year or two. Make a pile of money, blow it on an expensive apartment and eating out all the time, then move on and more of the same. Seattle, Boston, Miami for a short minute.

There was nothing fashionable about Iowa. Nothing sexy. But sitting in that bar with Sue I was starting to see the appeal of sincerity. Trees. Of people really not giving a fuck.

Sue recognized me. Not because we knew each other, but because we grew up the same: our rooms, our plates, all that had been the same size; we detassled in the summer; had the big, looming sky hold us accountable. She got it, all of it.

My mother used to call me every Sunday. Every Sunday I'd hear her voice and know she was talking only to me.

"What about your phone number?" I said when Sue and I were dividing things up. The landline was her business number. "How will you get jobs?"

"Same way I do now," she shrugged. "Just paint over the signs and spray a new tag."

"We can transfer the number."

"That seems like a lot of work," she said.

—

So far, I'd managed to fill three hours driving the back bowels of Cedar Rapids: the alleyways behind Zin's; Ellis Park with its massive flood wall; the shuttered A&W stand; the back retaining wall at Oak Shade Cemetery; the Rath plant with its enormous clouds of steam. I was looking for large, clear walls. Away from cameras, but not far from foot traffic. Places where you could hide, but your work could be seen.

The only other time I'd done something like this was in my teens when I had friend, an older friend, who'd ride freight trains around Iowa. We met outside Tobacco and News. He sat down on the stoop to roll a cigarette while I was playing hacky sack. Then I flubbed my turn and walloped him in the head.

"Is it like that?" he said.

Chuck was a little sideways. The sort of guy you'd never really take around in public because he'd steal drinks, backpacks—always lifting something, then disappearing for days, weeks at a time. We never knew how old he was. Twenty-five? Forty?

Once, just once, he tried to make a plan. Said he'd be riding through on Saturday night and could I pick him up at the railyard? There was a party on the southwest side, and if he walked all the way there he'd be sweaty. There was someone he wanted to impress.

I knew he'd be sweaty and smelling like oil from riding in a boxcar all day, so there wasn't a worry about being fresh. I wondered if the girl he wanted to impress was me.

I brought Tasha, dear Tasha, and we drove as near the railyard as we could get, down rutted roads, through unlit underpasses. We were in the middle of town, but it was dark like country, industrial country: a spooky haze over everything.

We were young and in a car. If you wanted to talk to someone, you just did. Every person we saw passed out by a tree, in a bush, we whispered: Hey Chuck! Oh, have you seen Chuck?

We finally gave up and went to the movies, *Truman Show*, maybe. We didn't know where the party was, and didn't care. It was hot, and driving around like that just made me want to go inside and wash my hands.

Three days later, there's Chuck outside Tobacco and News, talking like we'd just seen him that morning.

"Oh," he said. "Train didn't stop that run and I ended up all the way in Dubuque. There's no telling."

I saw him once or twice more after that. Then never again.

—

I took pictures of the tags I found and posted them on Instagram, then checked and rechecked my phone to see who liked it, who commented.

Maybe I'd get a tip on another tag, I thought, checking again. But really that wasn't it at all.

Sue didn't have a cell phone.

I sat alone in my car and stared at my phone, willing it, making bargains with it. Waiting for a direct connection.

—

I parked at the West End Tap, forty minutes from home this time of day. I'd never been here, but I'd driven past for years. How does that happen? You get attached to somewhere you've never even been.

It was a windowless hallway of a bar, with the bar on one side and very small tables on the other, plus a pool table and a jukebox. You could fit maybe thirty people in the whole place.

I didn't notice at first. Just ordered my vodka lemonade and took out my phone. It wasn't that my phone didn't work; it wouldn't even turn on. I tried again and again, then looked up.

There were four people at the bar, and none of them had their phones out. One woman looked at me and smiled.

"They don't work in here, honey. Dan put some sort of blocker in the ceiling makes 'em do that."

"Is that legal?" I said.

"Sign's on the door," she pointed. Sure enough, there was a sign right when you walked in. *Phones are disabled upon entering. Not responsible for damages.* And then, in larger letters: *Fully responsible for your good time!*

"It's her first time here," the woman said to the bartender.

"Welcome," he said, laying down a napkin, a quarter, and what looked like pudding in a to-go dipping container. "Newbies get a complimentary pudding shot and a song on the jukebox."

"They're good today," a man at the end of the bar said. "Last week they were mint." He stuck his tongue out.

"You still took it," the barman said. The man nodded.

I never got anyone's name. It was the sort of group who all knew each other, and maybe none of them knew each other's names either. It was the sort of place where things like that didn't matter.

I drank vodka lemonades. Played Dwight Yoakum tunes on the jukebox. At some point the bartender brought out a crockpot of little smokies and that was dinner.

I told everyone about what I'd been doing, about the graffiti tags, but they were more interested in the route I'd taken, making me talk it through, turn by turn. Everyone knew a different layer of town history, so I'd say Nelson's Meat Market or Olive and 7th and listen to them peel my travels back like an onion.

"What are those things?" the woman finally asked. "Those things you were chasing?"

"I've got pictures," I said, grabbing my phone out of habit.

"Just draw one out," a man said. "I got a pen."

I tried putting one on a bar napkin. I did the font, the stylings. I tried to get it just right.

The bartender set the bar phone in front of me for a model: a stumpy, ancient thing with a rotary dial and handset so heavy, so right, it could have been a weapon.

"Give it here," the woman at the end of the bar said. She stretched out her hand like someone had just called, like she wanted a turn.

How did I get here? I thought, leaning way over to her, the cord pulled tight. Whose number did I even know by heart?

"Just listen to that," she said, humming in tune with the dial tone. "Doesn't that sound make you homesick for something?"

Rules

The plan was for me to come straight over after work, but you know how it goes. You get home, change, and then there's the cat, and the mail, and you want to run the sweeper once and have a snack. But Tyler's the same way, so he gets it. I made it over closer to seven, with some Triscuits, a log of summer sausage, and a bottle of Jack. The garage was open, so I just went in.

It's a good-sized garage—a three stall with a bar and a big screen in the back. Tyler always keeps the far door open when I come over, and we treat that garage like a front porch, watching the neighborhood until we get cold and move over to the other side closer to the house. I knew he'd just been out there. There was a Honda CB750 up on blocks. The propane heater was on, the stools turned out, the camping chairs set. Tonight it was about forty degrees— perfect for standing around, smoking and drinking. Coming in here felt like going over to a friend's house when you're ten: walking into a basement with a ratty sofa and that slightly musty smell. Here's our space, here's all the time in the world. You can finally just be.

Last week's snow had nearly melted, but I still wore boots

over and brought a change of shoes for inside. Before I went in, I stomped my boots off in the garage, then took my slippers out of the plastic bag stuffed with snacks and booze. Tyler always razzed me about bringing slippers over, but I knew how much this house cost him and Rachel to build new. I wasn't about to track dirt all over it.

It was something that stuck with me from childhood, from the years I lived with my grandparents. I'd get up in the morning and come downstairs to sit by the heating grate, and Grandpa would say: Where are your slippers? You got to have your feet covered in this house. Their place was over a hundred years old and drafty, so we'd spend most days in the living room or the kitchen, and just go upstairs to sleep. Every year they'd have me pick out a new pair of slippers from the Lehman's catalog, the warmest ones I could fit into. That's what I buy today. They still feel good.

Tyler and I used to fool around, about a million years ago, back when we first met. This was before he was married, before I met my girl. I wouldn't call it dating, because we never went out to dinner or did things like that. I came over here once to a party and just never left. He came over to my place to help hang a door. And there was one time after work. But that was it. The way we were was never about settling down. It was more an extension of an early friendship. That's how I saw it, anyway. Tyler may have seen it different. But what it came down to was when he met his wife at a bar, I was happy for him. Things turned off, moved on.

"Where you at?" I opened up the door between the garage and the house. "You in here?"

"We don't want any!" he yelled back.

—

We were unattended tonight, I joked when I invited myself over. The governor was stopping through town for a rally at the convention center, and Tyler's wife Rachel and my girl Lexi went out to meet him. There wasn't supposed to be a big crowd, so the girls would get to shake hands and maybe have a little one-on-one time with the woman herself. Rachel and my girl are all about education, and they come at it from different angles: Rachel's a resource teacher at the local Catholic school, and my girl's a counselor at the alternative school. People are shocked they're friends, but people are idiots anymore: no one talks to each other. Rachel and Lexi love showing up at stuff like this, talking about how many youth development initiatives they've pulled off, how well they work together—just trying to get people thinking about new ways to move forward. They figured it was worth a shot. Governor Berger is a hugger, so at least they'd have a second or two near her ear.

Rachel brought her and Tyler's son along, too. It's good for kids to see how this all works, she always said.

Now that we both had women, it seemed like we never got time alone together. Tonight, I thought, we could actually talk. Actually get drunk. Have an evening to ourselves.

I come in and Tyler's sitting on his kitchen floor on an overturned five-gallon bucket from Home Depot. He's got an ARX160 Beretta half assembled in his lap, and the floor is covered in crushed cardboard and parts. I can see two boxes of ammo behind him. Every available flat surface—the counters, the table—is covered in dishes, Kinnick's homework, papers, mail, and books. Rachel's started making rosaries, and the kitchen table is a mess of eye pins and Job's Tears. The rest of the house was spotless, but his kitchen—like mine—was a dumping ground.

"It's not loaded," he said, pointing the rifle down. I trusted him, but with all that mess, I somehow didn't quite believe him. Anything could be anywhere in that kitchen. "You want to hold it?"

I grew up with guns, but in a different way from Tyler. My mother's brother took me out hunting ever since I was about seven. He started me with ducks because there was a lot I could do. I could paddle. I could feed the dog. I could blow the whistle. And I could just sit quiet and listen, just watch the sky and the water and feel the early morning air.

I loved every piece of it. When you're a kid, you're hungry for responsibility. For things you can manage and control. I ate up all the tricks my uncle could teach me. I knew if it was me who was in charge and not my perpetually unemployed father, my forever here and gone mother, I'd be set on my own two feet.

By ten I was shooting my own Remington, and by twelve I could taxidermy right alongside my uncle. "You got tiny fingers, that's good," he'd say. "Good strong, small hands." Then he'd show me how to paint the bill.

"Rachel ran out of here like a tornado, this kitchen is such a God damn mess," Tyler said, lifting a pile of dishes and putting them in the sink. But we didn't do anything to clean. Just left it all right there.

The Beretta came in the mail that day, and Tyler wanted to get right to it. Looking at the thing, I couldn't blame him. It's a very cool piece, with flip-up sights, and a folding stock for folks like me with short arms. I held it against my shoulder and looked around the house.

Tyler has two safes: one for long guns, one for hand guns. He's a collector, like his dad and his grandfather and who knows who else before that. Some of these guns are crazy old—just beautiful, preserved things that make you forget you're in your buddy's place and feel like you're in a museum, holding something important.

That's how he grew up, with safes and weekends trips out to the range, or to his aunt Marty's property. His aunt, from the sounds of it, was a little more like where I came from. She had two Remingtons: one above the door, one under the bed. She shot squirrels, raccoons, anything that annoyed her or that she wanted to eat.

"I brought snacks," I said, giving him back the Beretta. I went over to the drawer and took out a knife and a cutting board.

Tyler rustled through the bag and set everything out, then went to the fridge and pulled out two pears and an apple. I love pears.

We sliced everything up and ate it standing at the counter, right in the middle of all that chaos. Tyler kept an old boom box on the counter, one we'd take out in the garage with us later. I turned it on to KMRY—they do an Elvis call-in show on Friday night, where you win prizes if you can answer trivia questions about what was in the morning paper.

"I love this shit," he said, turning it up. "Like traveling back in time."

I put the Jack in the cabinet.

There were rules at Tyler's house, and this was part of the reason we were such good friends. Because we had the same rules, and we didn't have to say them out loud. If a gun's out, alcohol stays in the cabinet.

Compared to me, Tyler grew up with money. Two parents, still married, and a house so big it had bedrooms no one slept in. All his aunts and uncles still lived in Zwingle, or worked shift work in Anamosa, but his mom and dad were the ones in their families who wanted something different. They moved to Cedar Rapids and got degrees where they could make money—his dad's a CPA and his mother's an actuary. No matter the market or the president, there would always be numbers.

His parents didn't like it, but Tyler stayed close with the country side of things. He liked learning the old recipes and driving the four-wheeler out at his aunt's. Liked learning to dance the old steps.

We only talked about where we came from when we were together like this—not at work. Another rule. Working at Zinc was good most days—this web design company in a shiny factory over-haul in downtown Cedar Rapids. But it was also exhausting. Tyler worked in sales and marketing, and I was over in customer service. He had them at the beginning, I had them after they were hooked, or once they were pissed, or when they were ready for an upgrade. The same sorts of issues: how to talk to people about something they knew nothing about; how to teach people you never met how to do something abstract.

But I liked it. Working two floors down from the pool tables and the free beer, away from the engineers and all that, was the job equivalent of standing in the garage while everyone else is in the house. You're close to the action, but far enough away to have some distance, some freedom.

—

Tyler went to put the gun in the safe. Then he met me out in the garage with the bottle of Jack. I pulled glasses from the bar cabinet and found some Coke in the fridge.

"Did Rachel say anything to you?" he said, peeling off the seal. "Jesus, why do they make these so tight?" He flipped out his knife but I had mine first. I took the bottle from him.

"Pour it up," he said. "Rachel's going to take off. Go with Kinnick back to Colorado."

"For what? Visit her folks?"

"No, like to go."

He didn't say any more than that. Just took his glass and had a big swallow.

We stood there for a minute, looking out at the neighborhood. I could see the blue light of the television flickering at his neighbor's place, going from scene to scene. Why does television light look blue? When they were black and white, what did it look like then?

"She misses her family," he kept on then. "Says Iowa's not home. That I didn't make it a home for her, whatever that means."

He didn't look at me when he talked, just kept staring straight outside. "I might go too, I don't know," he said. "I could just be there, you know? Maybe we'll start a life out there."

"Is she divorcing you? Or she just wants to move?"

Tyler shrugged. "Something."

It was the look on him when he said it. Like he'd been left on the side of the road, like there he was, alone, watching his life drive away.

I couldn't imagine Tyler without his son, Kinnick. That boy was his light. Him living twelve hours away would break Tyler. It would make a good man desperate.

—

It wouldn't help Tyler's case for his wife to come home and find the two of us stinking drunk in the garage, throwing darts, but at this point I didn't figure it would hurt. She'd texted that the governor's plane was late, and while Tyler was on his phone I quick texted my girl: *Rachel's leaving Tyler maybe? WTF? You doing okay? We are drunk. Xo*

Conversation moved in circles. We'd start working on the muffler on the Honda, then walk away from it and start a bonfire in the yard, then walk away from that and start talking about Rachel while we smoked in the garage, or went inside for snacks, or just walked around the yard kicking along the retaining wall, talking about how this was the year we'd tear it all out and start over.

The boys on **KMRY** were pulling some deep tracks from Elvis. There was no moon. We were right here in the middle of the city, but sitting by the fire, surrounded by all that dark, felt like we were somewhere else. Away. Safe.

We sat there quiet for a bit. Tyler finished his drink and tossed the glass into the fire, lobbed it just right so it didn't break, just nestled there in the logs. Neither one of us said anything, just watched the glass crack in the heat and start to fold in on itself.

"You want to make out a little?"

"No, man," I said. "C'mon."

I quit drinking after that, just to keep an eye on things. It had been years, and he'd never once asked me that. Never once referenced the old days. Him saying that showed me his slide, showed me just how he was feeling without him having to say anything.

I wondered if he'd really locked up that Beretta.

I went inside to pee and instead of using the bathroom off the kitchen I headed through the family room, into the guest room with the large closet, the safes. I remembered the combination from a conversation years back. I don't think he meant to give it to me, but I held onto it, just in case.

No Berretta. Where the fuck was that?

I went back into the family room and looked around on the floor, beside the sofa, anywhere he might have tossed it. And there, tucked back on a bottom shelf, alongside some old DVDs, was the gun. *Why is he putting it there?* I thought.

"You ain't peeing," he said, walking into the room. "What are you doing?"

"We are drunk," I said, picking up the gun. "What are you doing?"

He flung his hands up and went into the guest room. So there I was with a Beretta that may or may not be loaded, and he's walking towards the room with the safes.

This isn't good, I thought.

I didn't go after him. Doing that, yelling something, would just make it worse. So I sat down on the sofa with the Beretta next to me. Just put my feet up like this was normal.

He came back into the room with a Glock 19, then sat down on the loveseat facing me. Set the gun down on the cushion next to him.

"There are rules," I said.

"Jesus," he said.

"What are we doing here?" I said, pointing my slipper at the gun.

Tyler wasn't Catholic, but he converted for Rachel. He went to mass every Sunday, did a week-long program for kids on outdoor survival skills at the vacation Bible summer camp, pressed a shirt every Sunday for mass. It wasn't about Jesus for him. He loved Rachel something fierce, would do anything to make her happy. There was a grace and steadiness about her that reminded him of the old ways, that filled him with a sense of purpose, security. He loved it. All of it.

"Sometimes I just sit in here at night. Just sit here and wait till I get my nerve."

The whole house was quiet. We still had the fire going in the backyard, I thought. The radio was on, the garage door open. Any second now they'd be home.

"You're talking about killing yourself."

He wiped his face. Put his head back on the sofa and looked up to the ceiling.

"You been thinking about that a lot?"

"Jesus, I just fuck everything up." He hit himself on the side of the head with his free hand.

I didn't want to change my energy, give anything away. Like when you're getting up on an animal, coming in. Once your heart changes, they know. And they'll fly.

"You're not leaving them," I said. Calm, steady. "You'll move together, or you'll figure it out and all stay here."

I kept on. "You haven't done anything," I said. "Is she just lonesome? Or what's she feeling?"

We weren't looking at each other. He was looking straight ahead, and I had my eye on the big picture window, the doorway beside. I could see whoever was walking in here.

"We'll take Kinnick next weekend, how's that? You guys get out of town, have some time."

He put his head in his hands and made a sound like he was about to throw up, like he was letting something out and swallowing something whole at the same time.

I got up then and made my way over. I touched his back. He'd sweated clean through his shirt, he was so alive right then.

"They're gonna be here any minute. Get in the bathroom, get yourself together."

I went for the Beretta first, carefully carried it back down the hall and put it back in the safe. Then I go to the loveseat for the Glock and it's not there. I stuck my arm down inside, pulled the cushions up, nothing.

There's a big full bathroom off the family room, all fancy with floor-to-ceiling tile. Tyler was standing up, looking at himself in the mirror. He had the Glock in his right hand, down at his side. The door was open, and I walked right in.

"They're home any minute," I said. "You gotta hold on."

When he didn't turn around, I tried again: "I won't tell anyone. I swear to God I won't ever tell anyone."

I positioned myself so I was there in the mirror. So my face was right next to his.

And then I put my arms around him, put my head between his shoulder blades. I just hold him. I put my hands on his chest like I did all that time ago. And as I'm smelling him and pressing him towards me, I can feel him fighting inside. How he wants to give in and relax back into me, but how he also feels like this is his chance. He's in the arms of someone who loves him. What a time to fly.

When you're standing in a tree stand, or sitting perfectly still in a boat, you have a lot of time to think. A lot of time to admire your surroundings: the stillness of the water, the sound of the leaves. Time to practice easing into that atmosphere, trying to disappear into it.

Everything around us was familiar, but now I was aware of it on a new level. The hum of the water heater. The cheerful sound of the furnace kicking in, the whoosh of hot air as it filled the passages and came breathing down on us from the ceiling vent.

"I love you so much," I said. "You know that? So much."

I moved my hand towards Tyler's right wrist, slid my fingers around it like a lover. I held on, thinking if I moved slowly enough, if I gripped his hand just right, I could make all of this—every bit of it—disappear.

A Record of Grief

1

Val left today to go camping up at Joy's. One of the Russians from their old dojo was visiting. She drove up mid-afternoon and called from the road—she'd pulled over—to let me know about an errat-ic driver who was all over his phone. "I called non-emergency," she said. "Total dipshit just weaving all over my lane." An officer from Waterloo was heading out to try and catch him. "He was just north of exit 8," she said. "Elk Run Heights."

Five people at a mall were killed in Dallas today. A shooter.

I mowed and trimmed, then Corner Ed pulled into the alley in his truck—on the way to Hy-Vee to pick up dinner. Talked about the neighborhood feral cats. After weeks of coaxing, I trapped the three-footed one and brought her inside. We'd have a long road with her. Ed and I talked about the heat, and fishing. He had the air running and the window down, but even leaning in like that I was starting to bake. Tapped the truck on the side and he drove off.

Went inside and read a Larry Watson book for a bit. I've read all the Longmire ones by now, but I forget the endings, so I can start them all right over again.

Turned into a perfect humid summer night. About eight I went for a walk—totally quiet. No one out. Streets are empty, doors closed.

Crossed 6th Avenue and saw police car 79. Waved because that's Phil's car, then remembered he'd be off shift by now. The officer didn't wave back.

Where is everyone?

Buddy was outside his house on a leash. He's so much bigger—coat looks good.

Oak Shade Cemetery had some action. Cars, motorcycles, one man visiting graves like me—recreationally.

I sat at the Hines burial plot—a stoned-off section at the top of a hill. It was a popular spot to sit and overlook the graves, the field beside, and the chain linked fence that sagged in the middle from deer jumping back and forth. I liked to sit at the corner, and so did other people. A can of Natural Ice and a wet empty pack of Newports were tucked in a gap between the stones.

The man looking at graves was still there when I left, and I took a different way back home in case he was eyeing me. Looked at flowers in other people's yards, trying to figure out what I could get to grow.

Text from Mark. Coffee at Java?

Their kids were at camp, so it was just him and his wife Anna. We drank coffee and she talked about some new jobs she was applying for. Mark and I talked about work, the rental he was fixing up.

When the shop closed we stood in the parking lot talking. The restaurant on the other side had a broken neon sign, so the word "steakhouse" flashed urgently.

Upstairs, the cat—I call her Biscuit—started meowing. When I got to the top of the stairs she peered out from one side, then stretched her front stump, like a pirate.

—

Like a lot of people, I grew up in Iowa, then left, then came back. Being from Iowa was the first thing I told people about myself. I felt I had to—I had to explain why I was the way I was, and "Iowa" was the fastest way.

I started in the south—a smooth transition out for a Midwesterner. After Atlanta came work in Pittsburgh, then Boston, then New York. I stayed in that time zone a long time, long enough to change my sleep schedule, my eating habits, my rhythm, my speech.

And I loved the new life, the new friends, the swagger I found. I stood tall without the modest Iowa shoulder slump. I lived out east so long that when I would drive back from visiting my family in Iowa I would see the New York skyline and feel I was home. Feel a sense of relief, that I could slip back into this fine jacket of a new life I'd built for myself.

But there came a point where I'd pull back into the city and feel like I'd outgrown that jacket. That I didn't want to put it on. It didn't fit anymore. My friends had gotten married, moved away for jobs, yards, second and third chapters. And I was ready for a transition too. Ready for some sky.

To start over.

—

I fear choices being made in my life not by me but by my indecision. That by putting off a choice long enough the choice would be made for me, not by me.

Control is my focus. For my wife, it's being right. We'd butt heads about it at the start of things—one person can't control the entire relationship, and no one is right all the time. Now we joke about it, like teasing each other about a food preference, or a love of ratty old shoes.

Val called in the morning to say she and her friend Joy and this Russian who was visiting were thinking about putting together a collective for the summer. There was a whole pack of visiting engineers up at the college for a summer conference, and she thought there was money to be made putting together some evening sessions for them.

"The guys in that Barkley marathon are always engineers. They love a problem, something physical to conquer."

"You'd put this together out at Joy's?" Joy had twenty acres outside of town.

That was the plan. Joy put in a free course years ago for anyone who wanted to come out and try it—tire run, adult-sized monkey bars, a rope net climb, all sorts of stuff. That would be the base, Val explained, then she, Joy, and the Russian would run different drills and exercises every day, leading up to a grand finale at the end of the summer—an intense, all-day competition.

"We came up with the plan last night around the campfire. I think it could work."

"Beer-fueled."

"Wine. Joy set up a meeting with the head of the department this afternoon, so we're typing up plans now."

My girl. Fearless.

"Do you mind if I'm up here for a while?"

"A couple weeks?"

"At least a month, to see this through. There's money, though, she said. "These guys totally all have money."

I'd go up on Mondays, we decided. Stay a night. Or she'd come down here. Monday would be their off day, with a four-pack weekend of course drills.

I was on a ten-month contract from work, so I was home. Picking up freelance here and there, and taming a feral cat. I could have gone up too. Maybe most people would have. But we liked having our own space, our own adventures.

56 people were shot in Chicago this weekend. One of the dead—21 dead— was a 4-year-old boy who was playing on his back porch.

I work in sales for event planning. I book the clients, create the packages, then turn them over to a manager who oversees all the nuts and bolts for the event. I'm the finances and the structure – none of the drama. When I transferred here, I argued for a ten-month contract, saying I could book more than enough clients during that time to keep us busy for the whole year. And I was right.

Part of the reason I came back was I was tired of the long hours, the drama, the headaches and bloat that came with this sort of hustle. So this time around, starting fresh, I wanted to see about doing it right.

I planned to power wash the siding. I drove over to Mark's to borrow his—it's gas-powered, and we took it out in his driveway to play with it.

"You gotta wear shoes with this," he said, holding it up. "I did this once in flip flops and damn near took my toes off. Just ate through those things."

We sprayed his siding, then wrote our names and drew some nasty pictures in his driveway before blasting them off.

After I moved back to Iowa I fell in love. Then, a year later, went through a rough break up. I didn't allow myself to drink alcohol for six months because I knew if I started I wouldn't stop.

Control. I couldn't control my heartbreak, so I took the reins on something else.

It got to be a different sort of routine. Come home, make dinner, watch television. Wish I could start drinking. Go to bed.

After a while life starts to feel like a long leash. This again. Over and over.

"Why don't you buy a house?" my friend David, back in the Bronx, said over the phone. "You can get a homestead or something," he laughed. But seriously, he said. A house would give me a project, something to keep my mind, my hands busy.

"I mean, your life sounds terrifying, with all those birds and raccoons just ready to attack." David was city through and through. Of all my friends, David was the one I knew would never leave the city. "But houses must be cheap out there, right? Get something you can work on."

So I did. I bought a 100-year-old two-bedroom place for $580 a month. That was my entire mortgage payment—insurance, taxes, everything. It needed a hug. I needed something to do.

The house kept me moving. I deleted my social media accounts, dumped all our letters. I'd been following my old love online, rereading letters, revisiting, thinking maybe, someday, how it could all happen again. Enough.

I took down wall paper. Refinished floors. Put in a new kitchen countertop. Cleaned out long neglected flower beds.

There was always something to do, something that needed to be done. A reason to get up, get outside. Something to borrow, something to share.

Four people were shot at a UPS facility in Detroit. A fired employee came back and burst into a management meeting.

Mark came by later on his way home from Menards. We got beers from the garage fridge and walked around the house, looking at the siding. His wife didn't get the job she'd applied for, so we leaned against the tailgate of my car in the garage, looking out at the alley, talking about jobs, insurance, what they might do so their oldest could get braces.

I told him about Val: the plan and the course.

"She's crazy, isn't she?" he said. "I wish I had the balls to do something like that."

My wife is not afraid to hustle. She's worked so many different jobs, and that was one of the things that attracted me to her. When we met she was working as a wine rep, but before that she worked part-time at a liquor store and part-time at a gas station.

She'd left Iowa and come back too, but her return landing was rougher. Her career away had been in construction, and she built a nice life for herself in Chicago. But she got sick of working for someone else, building someone else's ideas. Iowa was a good place for a hard reset.

"Work is work," she said. "I met good people at the gas station. And I learned things. And I got to try new things out."

When we got together and she moved down here, she did wine sales and set up a small construction shop in our second garage, just to start playing around, to start thinking about what she might do next. (It's not a second stall. It's a second, stand-alone garage. All Iowans dream of outbuildings.)

I came home one day and found her lying under what looked like an eight-by-four-foot metal helix.

"So this," she said, leaning up. She loved old playground equipment, but it was hard to play on once you got over four feet tall. So why not make some for adults?

We could climb on top of it, or underneath it, or try to test your balance and walk on it—it was three feet off the ground.

She took some pictures, started a website, then made more—a honeycomb jungle gym, an octagon filled with a climbing rope net—and set them up at Joy's.

My girl got a booth at local youth soccer tournaments where she showed off photos and models to parents. If their kids were active, maybe their parents would be too—or would aspire to be. She connected with Volley's, the adult beach volleyball league; the bikes and brews organization; the local community theatres.

It didn't take long for things to take off. She started making custom adult sized playground equipment, then American Ninja Warrior obstacles. People came from all over. Where else would you get eight-foot tall monkey bars in Eastern Iowa?

Then business expanded. Surprisingly it wasn't a far leap from creating exercise equipment that can sustain a 250-pound man to crafting custom BDSM suspension bed frames and harnesses. That's where the real money came in.

Last year she quit sales and started doing this full-time.

When your overhead's low, the sky's the limit.

—

I climb into bed and leave the windows open. It's so quiet here, is always what strikes me. In the cities I lived in, I'd always keep the windows closed at night, no matter how high up I lived, because it was so noisy. Ambulances running, cars moving down below, other people's air conditioners just rattling away. Just that dull hum that never stops. I'd turn fans on, or blast the A/C, to try and drown it out.

But here I leave it all open. I can hear the crickets, the cicadas. I can hear my neighbor Maureen talking with her mom on their porch across the street. I can lay here in bed and listen to them laugh, listen to them talk about the band that played up at the park, the other neighbors they hate, listen to them veer off into high, incomprehensible titters as they finish each other sentences and drink wine.

Sometimes when I can't sleep I'll walk through spaces I used to know well in my mind. Old apartments, or a friend's house from grade school. I'll move slowly, trying to remember pieces of furniture, smells, sounds. What it felt like to stand in this room. Where did I usually walk, what was the view like from this corner.

One of my favorites lately has been trying to walk through the Bishop's buffet line in my mind, starting with the roller-coaster style lineup area that snaked the crowd back on itself. The railings, I remember, were a twisted brass, like a thick metal rope. There was the choice of napkin. But the order to the food baffles me. Did Jell-O come before or after the side salad? Was pie really before the main course? How did a place with round wooden tables and big chairs on casters not feel like a nursing home?

Moving this way, I always end up remembering some forgotten detail, and the memory gives way to sleep.

Early the next morning I'm outside on the deck in my robe, watching Zorro and Bruce, two more feral cats, eat breakfast. I stay out there with them because sometimes this time of day the raccoons are still out, and I don't want one coming by and pushing them off their food.

I'm quite a sight, I think, sipping coffee. During my work months I'm in designer slacks, tailored jackets. I'm up late Sunday night ironing for the week. I shine my shoes, I smell good.

I don't even remember when I got this robe. Ten years ago?

Is one person more me than the other?

I'm heading into Beaumont today to visit family. I grew up there, on a block of tall, narrow houses packed together like a mouth with too many teeth.

After my mother died when I was twenty and away, my father moved into this rambling 1960's five-bedroom number off Wisner Road. It was just him, but he had always loved that house, always wanted to live there, so screw it. To him, the place still felt modern, like he had finally made it and nabbed the prettiest girl in the class after all these years.

The house had never been updated. The kitchen looked like a spaceship: Frigidaire Flair oven, dark cabinets with ornate handles, urine-yellow glass light fixtures. There was wood paneling all over the living room, a huge dark fireplace.

But the basement was the prize: a full bar with a complete barbeque kitchen, including a wall oven in the brick and a bright red fridge. A piano came with the place, and when he first got settled I came back out and we had a party. My sister played piano, we sang old songs, and we used the bar. The house was too big, it was ridiculous, but we all had a place to stay. And it sure was fun.

Dad got remarried to a woman twenty years younger, a nice Beaumont woman who liked to garage sale and craft. But when my father started to get sick, she just couldn't handle it. Or handled it in her own way. She went to sales all the time, bringing home boxes of old wicker baskets, furniture from the 1940s that was chipped or stained. A lot of it was just junk. She turned the old attached beauty shop, which had been sitting empty, into an antique shop of sorts, but really it was just for show. She was only ever open a few hours a month, and the prices were crazy.

So here's what my father did. He changed his will without telling any of us. Susie, my stepmother, could stay in the house after he died for one year. After a year the house and everything in it had to be sold, and the profits split between her and us kids.

By the time he was home dying, the only rooms you could access were his bedroom, the bathroom, and part of the kitchen. All the other rooms were stuffed full. The basement was completely inaccessible—we hadn't seen that bar in years.

He loved her, and he didn't want her to live like that.

A month after his death we had the first sale, and every other week after that we've been having sales and dumpster parties. And now we're starting to get somewhere. Moving slowly helped Susie;

enlisting the help of her friends, our extended families. Now I can walk through the rooms and turn around easily. It makes me happy. It makes me sad.

Grief will grab you. It'll hit you in different ways.

When my mother died I was out in Atlanta going to school, working nights at a restaurant. She'd always asked about the tourist spots—if I'd been to the Coca-Cola museum, if I'd been to a Braves game, or the Olympic park. I never went anywhere. I didn't have time, I didn't have the money, and it was so uncool to do those things. I was very concerned then with being cool.

But after she died, I started going. First to one place a month, then two, then as many as I could. I found myself exploring small museums and landmarks in my neighborhood: stopping to read the plaque beside the basketball court, the sign outside the house on the corner.

My mother loved history. She knew the names and stories of the founders of Beaumont, the stories about what bar used to be where, where the shooting ranges, bowling alleys used to be.

We'd go for walks and she'd whisper gruesome stories that took place in different houses: how in the big house on the corner of Sixth and Franklin the man killed his wife in the kitchen with a knife. Or how the rambling old white house on Bluff used to be a boarding house, and a man killed himself with a shotgun in the backroom.

I kept that strange tradition. Each city I moved to I'd research one or two notable deaths, then make a point of walking by where it took place. I'd add the houses, the parks to my walking routes, look up at the windows, watch the paint colors change, the landscaping, as owners changed. I told my mother stories in my mind as I approached. I could hear myself whispering to her. It was right at the top of the stairs, can you see it there through the window? That's where he pushed her.

I knew my mother one way as a kid, and now, as an adult, I like to imagine a different sort of relationship with her. Not as she was then, faded into the background of the house. But like a companion, an equal.

Who tells all these murder stories to their children?

I missed a lot there, I knew.

The sale was from nine o'clock until three o'clock, but the biggest crowd always came between eight and nine in the morning. Sometimes earlier. When I pulled up at a little before eight, Susie was sitting out front on an old folding chair holding a baseball bat.

"They keep trying to get in!" she said.

I kissed her on top of her head and tried to take the bat away. She pulled it towards her, and I let go.

"Is the coffee on?" She jerked her head back towards the kitchen.

Having these sales so often turned into a grand excuse for a family party. Members on Susie's side I'd never met now I found myself looking forward to seeing. There were two Mr. Coffee's burping on the counter, and a large tinfoil container of coffee cake. My sister Cathy brought some Hawaiian Rolls from Fareway, and there was a big Tupperware container of Chex Mix on the island.

There were eight of us today, plus Susie. I ended up being stationed in the old antique shop with my nephew Ethan, who was sixteen.

I patted Ethan on the back as we made our way through the garage and into the shop. "Your first time doing this?"

"First time," he said. Ethan was a rail thin blond kid with green eyes. Tall, too. Six feet at sixteen.

He picked up a rubber trinket gone hard with time. It was a stiff, now-brown fish holding a small pole. "Gone fishing," it said underneath.

"Are we selling this? This stuff's nasty."

I took it from him and tucked it behind a pack of Precious Moments from the '90s. "Cheap."

"Garbage," Ethan said, crossing his arms. "I'm going to live in a tiny house."

Susie only came to check on us twice the whole day, thankfully. She was so busy in the garage she just turned the rest of the property over to the family. We spent the day trying to peddle crap people either already had or didn't want: full sets of glasses, witty figurines from the '80s and '90s, country music cassettes, a shot glass collection from the Rocky Mountains.

But Susie would walk around and lovingly touch everything, hold an old vase up to the light and admire it through the dust.

There was something strangely beautiful about the pride she took in this junk: what she could see that I couldn't, what she could feel that I didn't.

Things quieted down and we got some lunch—someone ordered a bunch of Subway sandwiches, and there was a never-ending supply of Pepsi in the fridge. Ethan and I sat together behind an old glass counter in the shop and ate.

I asked him to tell me everything he had in his bedroom. Did he have it packed like this? What was in it?

In his room:
    A single bed with a red comforter and black sheets (school
    colors, he shrugged)
    Bookcase full of sci-fi, fantasy novels
    Dresser with speakers and a docking station
    Lava lamp
    4-H trophies

Small cactus on bedside table

I knew what Ethan's room looked like: in most houses it would be a nursery, or a large closet. But he never complained. If it's all you know and it's all yours, there's no problem.

"What's your favorite thing in there?"

He chewed his sandwich, then swallowed. "The cactus. I'd take that if I had to take one thing."

"Not your phone?"

"Well, yeah, my phone, but that's always on me. I'm thinking like what's in my room and stays in my room. The cactus."

"You love it."

"Yeah. It's alive. It's cool."

Yesterday there were two mass shootings in the United States, where four or more people were killed. All of these events were perpetrated by men, explained Richard Jones, a panelist on Fox News. Yet there are no programs in place in the United States to help men learn how to control their emotions, to channel anger, disappointment, fear, away from violence. These are not things men are allowed to discuss in our society. The rest of the panel, all men, looked visibly uncomfortable as he went on.

I drive outside Beaumont and stop at St. Joseph's Church. It's an old farm church, out in what looks like the middle of nowhere. Just farm fields as far as you can see, then at the top of the hill this big brick church and a rectory. And trees. Lush old burr oak trees. There aren't trees for miles—just wide-open sun bake—and these old guys and their shade look plain luxurious.

I like to pull over here if I'm tired, if I need a break before driving all the way back home. A cool spot to nap. I've never once gone in to pray, but sometimes I pray out here in the car.

I call Val. They've got the course assembled, and today they're just working on the schedule. The plan is to have participants train on the different obstacles, leading up to a timed race at the end of the month. But instead of racing on the obstacles, Val and Joy came up with something more interactive.

"We'll start everybody at different spots," she explained. "We're thinking six laps around the property? Start around six in the morning so they'll get the full bake by the afternoon. Oh, get this. Joy got Farmer Jeff on board and in each lap the guys will have to detassel four rows of corn. Free detasseling!"

"Jesus."

"We're calling it the sun-bake challenge. Detasseling, rappelling up and down that old silo, breaking sod with a hand tiller. It's awesome. The engineers'll train on all the playground equipment so they think the race will just be through the course, but then they'll have to do all this new stuff. They're going to shit themselves."

The plan was to have each participant pay a couple hundred for the training sessions, but make the final race really cheap. Take a page out of the Barkley book: folks are less likely to sue if the experience only cost a couple dollars.

"You'll come up for the race."

"Sure. Put me in charge of something. I'll bring sunscreen."

My wife and I talk on the phone a lot, but when she's gone for a period like this I also write her letters. It makes it so I feel like she's with me more often. We did this when we were first dating, when we were long distance. I'd think about her during the day, think about what I'd write to her, how I'd tell the story to make her laugh. I'd send her postcards. Small, handmade things with short messages. We lived in different towns and talked on the phone every night, saw each other once or twice a week. But sending something in the mail felt sexy, forward. Why stop now?

By the time I got back to the house the neighbors had lawn chairs in their backyard, and they'd moved their outdoor tables—two man-sized wooden spools used for holding electric cables—into the center. A white sheet hung from the roof, over their kitchen window, to act like a screen for the projector.

"We're doing an 80s night, if you want to stop over," Kathy said when I got out. "Double feature of *Sixteen Candles* and *Karate Kid*."

I was in. They'd done this before, sometimes with a bonfire at the same time. Their friends and family would come over, folks we'd sometimes never met, and you just get to sit all together and laugh and joke through the movie everyone's already seen a million times. Plus drink.

I checked on Biscuit upstairs. She'd been sleeping on the bed, I could tell, because there was fur everywhere. But now she was hiding under the bed, glaring at me. I put some food in her bowl, changed the water, and went back downstairs.

After the movie, it was late. I took a piece of cardboard out of recycling, then cut the crossword and the Jumble out of the day's paper and pasted them on.

You fill in the missing pieces, I wrote, then addressed it to Val.

2

I was out at Theisen's the next day when it first happened. I was walking
through the gardening hand tools, eating my free bag of popcorn,
when I caught a glimpse of someone. I didn't see a face, or anything that would be recognizable. But there was a feeling. It felt
like my mother. Like she'd just passed from one aisle to the other.

A tracksuit. My mother would never in a million years wear a
tracksuit.

But as a walked down the aisle, picking up hand tillers, spades,
gloves, I felt it again. And then there she was, older, with long hair
pulled back.

Mom?

I wanted to weep but I was so confused. I knew she had died, had
seen her, held her, picked out clothes for her, put dirt on her. Mom
was dead.

You're dead, I said.

Duh. She smiled. Get your tools. I'll meet you outside.

And she was gone.

Who says duh? My mother never said that.

I went straight to the check out and got a Pepsi out of the cooler at the end of the lane. I started drinking it while I waited.

"How's your day?" the checker asked. There was no one behind me. It was Monday.

"Weird," I said. "I swear I just saw my mother, but she's been dead for fifteen years."

"In this store?" she said. She kept ringing up my items. "My friend saw her dead father driving down 380, damn near crashed her car. Your mom's considerate, showing up in a store."

Talking with strangers is one of the best things about moving back to Iowa. "It's spooky."

"It is spooky. I never believed in ghosts until my friend told me that. She never makes stuff up. She's a nurse, she's real sensible. But you never know, right?" She handed me my items in a plastic bag.

I walked slowly out of the store, stopping to look carefully at the fifty-pound bags of fertilizer, the baby chicks, the bins of animal feed. I loved the smell of this place: sweet animal feed, sawdust, the free popcorn machine popping away.

I was dawdling. She won't be outside, I told myself. Just leave. You can just leave.

Here was my thinking, my attempt at rationalization there in the Theisen's feed section: The brash, sloppy woman/ghost/whoever couldn't have been my mother—I must have misheard her—because she looked nothing like my mother. Acted nothing like my mother.

Mom had been a warm, kind woman who stayed at home with us. We had five acres just outside town, and growing up Mom was always out in the garden, working away on beans, tomatoes, carrots, beets. You name it, it seems like she grew it. She wore house-dresses, kerchiefs on her head. She built all sorts of contraptions with scrap from around the property to keep rabbits out, build up shade when she needed it. She'd cook and can and the kitchen would be a steamy mess on those days. I remembered her arms, tanned in the summer, the skin under her biceps waving as she mashed potatoes.

It was an older time in my house. My friends had cereal for breakfast, mothers who worked. We had fresh eggs, pancakes. Hot dinners every night. The house was spotless. Our clothes were ironed.

But here was my other thought, my larger, more curious/terrifying/unknown thought: the tracksuited woman felt like my mother. A feeling came off her like a wave, a smell, a view I hadn't seen in years that was intensely familiar. Like when I'd imagine myself walking through Jenny Crosby's basement, my old childhood friend, and remembering the wall phone we used for prank phone calls, the smell of her downstairs laundry room where we'd have our most personal conversations, putting our sneakers in the dryer so her brothers couldn't hear us over the thumping, then putting on hot shoes, the metal lace tips of my Keds leaving small hot circles on the tops of my feet.

It's that wash of nostalgia, love, belonging, gratitude, all wrapped up together. It hit when I saw her.

What was this?

You need something to do, Mom said. She was there, walking me to my car. You still have this piece of shit? I know you can buy something better.

Mom, I said. I knew it was crazy, but I believed. I wanted to. It was a dream, I thought, and I may as well experience it fully. What is wrong with you? You don't swear.

I don't smoke either, she said, lighting up a cigarette. She got in the passenger's seat then, just appeared there, and snapped her fingers at me like, *Hurry up*.

We didn't say anything as we drove back to the house. It was all I could do to concentrate on the road. Mid-morning summer in Cedar Rapids, Iowa, was not traffic central, but there were still people out. The Casey's was full of people filling up. Mr. Freeze had a few early kids on bikes, sitting at picnic tables, playing with their phones. A man in a Hoveround made his way down the side-walk.

We passed the library, the flower shop, the furniture refinishing store. When I turned down the alley for home, Mom disappeared, then was there on the stoop.

I parked and got out and sat next to her.

I figured this would be a good time, with Val being gone. I wish I could have met her, she said. I like her.

Really?

Yep. I like that you married her. Your father was sure slow to come around, wasn't he?

I shrugged. That was all a long time ago now.

A good time for what? I said.

She gave me a sad, closed-lip smile. You know. And I know. I know all of it, okay?

I stared at her. Her face was weathered like she'd been out at sea for years. I was starting to feel lightheaded.

I'm going back to bed, I said. I'm going to wake up and you'll be gone.

Mom blew smoke in my face. I could smell it. Clove cigarettes. They've been illegal in the U.S. for years. Something about kids smoking them.

Not a dream, she said. But I get it. Too much in one day? Too much. I'll go.

She moved her foot to the side and tapped it against mine, one, two. My mother wasn't real affectionate. She'd hold our hands and kiss our foreheads, but she wasn't one for hugging or crying or big displays of affection.

But when I'd be sitting next to her, or across from her, sometimes she'd stretch her foot out and tap mine, twice like this, and smile at me like we were sharing something. I'd forgotten that memory until that moment, and then it all came rushing back.

There I was, on my back step, crying in the sunshine.

3

After I pulled myself together, I called Val. I decided I wasn't going to tell her about my mother's visit. Or I would but not now, not yet. Give it some time to pass, to breathe. Then when I was stronger, I could tell the story better. A sort of "you wouldn't believe this, how weird is this," sort of story, instead of the emotional gut punch it was now.

"Hi, this is Val. You've reached my cell." I love her voicemail. I can tell, just from hearing her voice, that she's smiling. I picture her recording it standing outside—she always loved to be outside—with her hair short, parted to the side slightly over one eye. It's summer. With Val it's always summer.

"Hey, baby."

I miss her.

To clear my head I decide to head up to Coggon and do a float down the Wapsipinicon. There's a spot off the river outside of town where you can camp, get firewood, and rent canoes or kayaks. The guy will drive you up the river, drop you off, and then there's a call box at the landing point where you can ring him to come pick you up.

It was ten dollars for the rental and transport. Val always thought that was exorbitant. "All it takes is planning!" she'd say. If she went out, she'd lock the kayak up at the drop point, then drive back down to the end and leave the truck. Then she'd ride her bike up to the starting point so by the time she finished her float, she could just pop the kayak in the truck and drive back up and get her bike.

"Who wouldn't want a bike ride and a float?"

I wasn't up for logistics today. We had money. I'll spend ten dollars.

I waved the man off, then stood there covering myself in sunscreen while I watched him drive away. Once the sound of his tires on the gravel faded out, the birds and the trees bending in the wind took over. It was always so noisy out here, but in a different way, a soothing way that makes it so it doesn't even feel like noise. All the sounds just come together, like my breathing, my heart.

There's a catbird. There's a whippoorwill. There's a blue heron. Another one.

How long had it been since I'd done something like this?

Val would be thrilled.

Val died seven months ago, a week before Christmas. She was driving home from a client's house, down this woodsy two-lane road with lots of big homes tucked inside. In winter, when the trees were bare, you could see farther into the forest than you could any other time of the year. Just on and on.

She hit a patch of black ice and the truck skidded off the road, down a slope into the woods, where she hit a tree. The paper said later that the homeowners heard the crash—you make a big noise barreling down a hill in a truck, smashing into a tree—but no one went out to investigate. No one called it in.

It was only when the truck caught fire someone made a call.

I found out later that she could have survived the crash, but not the fire. That if someone had bothered to come outside, to make a call, to pull her out, she might have lived.

The officer who came to the house in the middle of the night didn't tell me any of this. He just bundled me up in a squad car and drove me to the hospital with the lights flashing.

Val was already gone when we got to there, but I was so out of my mind I forced everyone to keep running scans, to check everything they could think of.

She's tough, I said. There's no way. She's in there, she's in there.

All I could think about in the days and weeks after that was killing myself. Driving back out to that stretch of woods and ending it. My father, he was still alive then, seemed like he could smell it on me, so he told me to take family medical leave and come up and stay with him. We sat together, I dressed him, took him out to the mall where we'd walk up to the fountain, then just sit on the bench watching people until he was ready to walk back out to the car.

Mark knew it too. It was his idea about the cell phone. He asked me for it when we were planning the funeral. For the password, all of it.

"I'll keep it," he said. "I won't listen to the messages, but I'll clear her voicemail out every now and again. That way you can call whenever you want."

I made up stories about where she was. She would always be off on some adventure. It wasn't uncommon for us to spend time apart. I'd say she was out surfing in Northern Minnesota. That she was out at some BDSM convention selling her stock. Some of the stories, like her building the course with Joy, were pretty outlandish, even for her. But Mark always played along, let me brag about her, let me see her in my mind as alive, just off somewhere else, doing something exciting.

That she'd be home soon. It wouldn't be long. Just a little while longer.

By mid-February I'd gone back to work. Being busy suited me. Kept me moving. I left the house, her workshop, unchanged. I called her phone a couple times a day. Smelled her pillow. Opened up her dresser drawers and touched her old t-shirts.

By April I started thinking that having June and July off would be good for me. But Mark worried that having all that time to myself would be dangerous. Get a part-time job, he said. Or stay on here at work, just to have something. But I kept reminding myself how nice it was to get away. All the house projects I could get done. The floats and hikes and barbeque recipes.

When summer came around, the first few days were great. Then the calendar yawned open and I fell in.

You need a project, Mom said, appearing in the mud room. A positive project.

You're just sitting in the house, imagining all the things you could be doing, without actually doing any of them. You'd never go canoeing by yourself. You're not that fun.

I didn't know what to say, so I didn't say anything. I thought I had been doing pretty well, fooling myself, Mark, the neighbors.

You need someone you can't bullshit for a while, she said.

"If men in this country were 98% more likely to suffer blindness, we'd be forming research teams and taking action," the panelist explained. "But when they're 98% more likely than the rest of the population to perpetrate a mass shooting, we turn a blind eye." George Baker, another panelist, jumped in. "Don't you think you're being a bit dramatic?"

For the last two weeks I really hadn't been getting out of bed. When I did get up, it was just to go downstairs and eat cereal in front of the television.

But when I'd be in bed, with the feral cat tentatively making her way towards me, I'd imagine what I could be doing that day: visiting friends, walking down to the cemetery, over to the river. But really days would stretch into each other.

I started keeping a journal of what I did —or what I imagined I did. Just to keep the days straight.

When I looked back on the journal, I wouldn't be able to remember what was real and what I made up, I imagined the events so vividly.

The journal, this record, would somehow help me through.

I'd be remembering events, actions, activities, instead of myself lying on a dark couch in my PJs.

—

Mine had been an entirely different existence than Val, whose parents were abusive and neglectful, leaving her alone for days at a time—which she said she preferred to them being around, because it meant they didn't hit her and keep her up in her bedroom where her dad had nailed the windows shut.

Growing up was when Val got good with tools. She'd work small jobs and buy a hammer, a screwdriver, a pair of pliers at the hardware store. She could pull the nails out and put them back just right so her parents wouldn't notice. When they'd leave her alone for stretches she'd cook herself meals, then stockpile them in a cooler under her bed for when they'd come back.

"I thought about running away a lot," she'd say. "But what I really wanted was for them to just go away for good and leave me alone. I was fine. I went to school, I could cook for myself, I just wanted to be left the hell alone."

When her dad left her mother, Val was fifteen, and things got better. She and her mom lived like roommates, staying out of each other's way. When she was sixteen Val dropped out of school, got her GED, moved out to Arizona and started over.

"It's amazing I'm not dead. Or that I didn't kill somebody. That's amazing."

"The way to prevent and curtail tragedies such as these is to loosen restrictions regarding conceal and carry laws. If a wider segment of our population is trained and carrying, a perpetrator will think twice about opening fire on a group of citizens." The first commentator jumped back in. "That continues the cycle that violence is the only answer for men. It isn't."

Why can't you be Val? I asked Mom. We were sitting in the living room, drinking beers. I hadn't drank since Val left, but one with my mother, one with company, felt okay.

It's too soon for her, my mother said with a wave of her hand, like I knew what that meant. Besides, you need someone from outside your life now.

My life now?

Who you are now. You're different than you were as a kid, way better than you were in your twenties, no offense.

I shrugged. Totally right.

It was either going to be me or your grandpa Steve come down to see you.

My grandfather Steve died when I was six. I just had a few memo-ries of him: holding my hand, racing a plastic car across the dining room table, walking down the streets of Beaumont high up on his shoulders. I remembered he had a certain smell. I couldn't tell you the smell, just that there was one.

Why him?

My mother explained that it had to be a person from my group. These words aren't going to be enough, it's not quite the same, she said. But you've got a group—some family, some not—who are there for you. I'll call it a committee because that's a term you know, but it's not like that, not boring or official like that.

These people can't change or influence anything about your life, but they're there with you, they're connected to you as you go through it. Everyone's got a group like that. Even at your most lonesome here, you're still part of a collective.

Val's not in my collective?

Don't be all upset. It too early for her yet. And she might not be in it. She might just be with you on her own, like a free agent—you understand that.

So it was going to be one of us, she kept explaining. And we figured it'd be better if it was someone you actually sort of knew and had a connection to.

What's with the outfit?

This? She laughed.

When you're dead you do what you want. It's tough though because you think, why the hell didn't I do all this earlier? Now I learned how to drywall and do carpentry—always wanted to do that. Don't have to wear dresses, cook, none of that. And why not smoke? Can't hurt me none.

How long are you going to be here?

'Till you get talking, she said. We all know what you've been up to. So 'till we work this through and I know you're safe.

I didn't want to talk about anything. I felt a pit open up in my stomach: shame and fear and unbearable sadness. I visualized the feelings stuffed inside of an old steel footlocker. When the lid started to open, I pushed it shut. I would roll things on top of the locker, like a rock, or an anvil, to make sure it stayed closed. But little by little, the door worked its way open, again and again.

And then in my mind there was my mother, sitting on top of the rock on top of the footlocker, there in her track suit, smoking. She didn't say anything.

4

When I thought about acts of devastation, it was always hypothetically.
How the folks who did these acts were too emotional, too
untrained, hadn't thought through all the scenarios. I'd read an
article about a shooting at a mall and think: "Well, of course he
only killed two people. He'd never been to this mall before. He
didn't know his way around."

I'd never go as far as writing things down, or making a plan, or
something dumb like doing an internet search. Just kept it in my
mind. This wasn't something I thought about lying in bed when I
couldn't sleep—this is the sort of thing that winds you up. But if I
was in line at the check-out, or sitting outside waiting for a bus or
something: it was a way to pass the time. Entertain myself.

The more I thought about the violent acts, about how much damage could be done with a shooting, the more I realized that if the
goal was doing a lot of damage—of really striking fear—there
were better ways to go about it. Delivering poisoned baked goods
to offices; tainting soap dispensers, or the communal sunscreen
dispensers at the ball park. There were bigger results, bigger fear,
to be had if you were content to remain anonymous.

Men never liked doing anything anonymously. I had a chance, I thought.

I'd move between thinking about large-scale events—purely from a hypothetical, problem-solving perspective—to the most effective path to suicide. But the suicidal thoughts were never as—soothing is the wrong word, but it's all I can come up with.

With event planning, it was all about preparation, control. With suicide, there was none of that. The desire to end it would come over me like an attack, sometimes in bed, sometimes when I was at work, in the middle of a meeting with a conference room full of people. No planning or warning whatsoever. It felt like a wash in my head. An incredible urge would come over me to bash the right side of my head against something—the corner of the table, the wall, the glass window. And I'd have to stand there, palm sweating, my vision starting to black over, and pretend everything was fine.

I made the mistake of asking myself the question one day. If I was going to do it, how would I go? Unfasten the seatbelt and turn the wheel. Into oncoming traffic was best, I decided, because chances of failure were low. There're plenty of narrow, rural two-lane roads in Iowa, where people careen along at 65 mph. I didn't consider the other driver—what it would be like to witness something like that. Or what if I killed someone? When you're in a tunnel like that of just wanting to end everything, you can't see the other sides. The world is gone at that point. Tethers are cut. It's just about getting through the hole.

When a wave would come while I was driving it took everything I had to focus on my hands, to just keep them on the wheel and not turn in. Straight, straight, straight, I would tell myself. I would make that voice as loud as possible because I knew, in that state, it would take just one small break and I'd turn. When the impulse hits and you have everything you need, there's no stopping.

See, my mother said. She was sitting on my bed, her back against the footboard, her feet up by my head. She kept her shoes on. You could go a lot of different ways.

I didn't actually want to kill anyone. I didn't want to hurt any-one. What I wanted was for people to not take one another for granted. These married couples were so fucking lucky, I wanted to scream. She's right there next to you and you're on your phone? He just touched your shoulder and you're still scrolling Facebook? An illness, a small accident, something, anything, to jolt them out of this ridiculous reality and into paying attention—really paying attention—to one another.

I'd had an idea.

You know, my mother said. I'm not going anywhere. You need to watch yourself.

"It stems back to the perceived differences between men and women in this country," commentator Malcom Johnson said the following morning on The Chew. *"There's this notion that certain traits are more masculine or feminine, and that one shouldn't have traits that are opposite to their gender. But truthfully, scientifically and socially speaking, to be healthy we need a balance of both." "No one calls you a bitch when you're tough," Sara Gilbert said. "That's right. And no one calls you a pussy when you feel bad about something."*

I'd been thinking about a big wedding coming up at the hotel for 300. I booked the event back in January, just after Val died, and pulled all the strings together for the couple: catering, sound, tables, lighting, the whole bit. It was a big package, a huge celebration, but the couple seemed detached. Like they were going through the motions. Like they were only in it for the photographs.

They picked the best of everything, but they did it independent of each other. There wasn't any talk about the actual wedding, or how all this would go together. It was just: I want this, and I want this. For the man it was the most expensive sound package, satin tablecloths, three meat dishes. And the woman wanted that stupid chocolate fountain that's just chocolate-flavored oil; a parquet dance floor; huge arrangements of live corn stalks around the room.

When Val and I got married, the focus was on the ceremony and building our life together. We did marriage prep classes, spent lots of nights talking about money, sex, kids, and what we wanted out of life—both individually and as a couple. The reception was an afterthought, a small luncheon with homemade pie and coffee. For the honeymoon we did a road trip through the Midwest, seeing favorite places we traveled to when we were first dating: Milwaukee, Door County, Chicago.

I understood that all relationships, all marriages were different. But Val and I did a lot of things right. We were good in so many ways. And she was gone and here was this couple, living day-to-day together, with no real appreciation for one another, not ever jumping into the deep end of the relationship.

I didn't want anyone to get hurt. But I was planning on having everyone in attendance get sick.

The conference center was on a separate heating system from the rest of the hotel, and the pool was directly underneath the Carver reception room. During the middle of dinner, when the room was at its fullest, I'd adjust the pool heater exhaust to release CO_2 into the room. I wouldn't go for long. Just long enough to make everyone dizzy, to make people sick. To bring a little panic, fear. Appreciation.

I know it's like playing with fire, thinking you can control a gas. But I'd been preparing.

I bought a gas mask from the military surplus store back in March, and once every two weeks I'd do a test run with it: opening the oven door and sitting on the floor in front of it, where the fumes were the highest.

The first time I tried it out I didn't know for certain the mask even worked. I thought, either this will work or I'll be found dead here on the kitchen floor with this mask on. I wrote a note out and left it in plain view on the kitchen table so if I died responders would think this was a weird suicide, not me planning some sort of event.

"It was time to go." The note said. "Cat is upstairs with windows open. Please rehome." Then I signed my name.

After practice I would box up the mask, my monitors, my levels, my notes, and store them in the crawl space underneath the dining room. I'd open all the windows and go for a walk, blocking every-thing out of my mind. I'd look at houses in the neighborhood, their windows all lit up and cozy in winter. I'd pay attention to the sound the snow made as I crunched or squished my way through it, depending on the amount of moisture in the air, the tempera-ture.

I'd slide back into my other self— my true self—and think about work, about what I was doing that weekend, about Val and how I missed her. The actions in the kitchen seemed like a dream, like when you wake up thinking something was true, then you realize it wasn't. The emotion, the fear might be true, but the action never took place. Wasn't possible.

Worked out today for twenty minutes, I would write in my journal. Getting stronger each time.

—

When I got out of bed, my mother was gone. I showered, dressed, and went downstairs for breakfast. The cat, Biscuit, was still pretty skittish, so I took my breakfast over to where she was sitting in the window and sat beside her. I haven't made to touch her yet. I just feed her, scoop her box, and sit next to her as much as I can. I read that somewhere, some old article about a circus trainer, when working with an animal the best way to earn its trust was to just sit with it. Don't force it.

It was another beautiful day—the clouds were the big Marvin Cone kind: so large and changing it was like they were alive. I rolled the windows down and pulled out of the gravel alley, turning onto 7th Street.

Ricky from the KMRY morning show was going on about a bad driver he saw on the S curve. At my lowest point I would sit in the house and listen to this man's entire morning show, sometimes from bed, sometimes while sitting on the kitchen floor. I've never met him, never seen him, but I'll always think of him as a close friend.

I drove up north, where all the new houses are coming in. Then I turned and did a lap through the prairie at Sartori Park, with the huge towering sculptures of reeds and grasses rusting overhead. Went up on County Home Road, out where the houses have bigger and bigger lots until they just give way over to farmland and open sky.

When Val and I were working on the yard we decided to turn a patch of it over to prairie. It used to cover the entire state, now it's regulated to small, carefully maintained park spaces. We wanted the yard to be a little wild, a little historic.

"Look at this shit," Val had said, tossing me a seed catalog. Hundreds of dollars for prairie seeds, for starter sets. "Seeds are free. I'll just go up to Sartori Park at the end of the season."

So we stripped down a chunk of the lawn, pulling up the sod, tilling the soil, and early one fall morning Val went up to the park with a brown paper grocery bag and just started taking seed heads willy-nilly from the prairie. She came home with huge, billowy clouds of milkweed, Death-Star coneflower heads, and handfuls of random seeds we'd have to plant to find out what they were.

She threw a handful of milkweed at me, those whisper-soft puffs. "Nature!"

We'd lived in this town ten years, and everywhere I turned there was a story, a memory of Val, usually involving her doing something wacky. Something people would initially say was a stupid idea not because it was but because it was so different, so fun, it caused people to be a little fearful. Could life really be that spontaneous? That free?

The summer before she died was idyllic. We went tubing down Indian Creek, right through Cedar Rapids. Went out to the lake at Palo for swimming, to Noelridge to do the slides. Val's business was growing but she kept her own schedule. I was off for the summer, which meant I could work in the yard, putter around town; we could schedule her work around our adventures. Free concerts in the park every Thursday night. Farmer's market downtown every Saturday. The days were hot and languid and filled with whatever we wanted them to be. It was a lucky, gifted life to be this flexible.

And then she was gone. And then.

Your father didn't love me the way you love Val, Mom said sitting down to lunch with me. Ever since she showed up I started craving foods we ate as kids: bologna sandwiches on white bread with Miracle Whip; Cheetos; Pepsi; fruit cocktail from a can. I sat down across from her with my spread and gestured to it.

Nah, I'm fine, she said. I'd never seen her eat in front of me yet. Looks good though.

Dad loved you.

In his way, she said. But for us it was different. More like an arrangement. We grew to love each other, we got real used to having each other around—we never spent a night apart. But it's one thing to miss someone because you love them and another to miss them because they've always been around. You know?

I took a bite of my sandwich, felt the crunch of the iceberg lettuce against the otherwise mush of soft bread and bologna. The sensation, the taste was great.

Your father had his issues, too, she said. We both did.

"Men and women are equal, but they're different," commentator Loretta Daniels said to Terry Gross. "Now I'm not saying they're treated equally, but in terms of ability, worth, strength, they're equal but different. But for a woman to gain ground in this country she needs to become apt at masculine tasks—we've seen this in everything from fashion to mannerisms to obstacles for ninja warrior. Instead of making women go to one hundred on the masculine scale and making men stay near zero on the feminine scale, we should encourage a balance on both sides."

"Like a left hand, right hand sort of thing?" Terry asked.

"Not even that, because one hand is dominant in that metaphor. Feet are a better metaphor. They do the same thing, want the same thing, but are slightly different. And when they move together, more gets accomplished."

Your father would have these bouts, even back when we first got married, where he'd just sit in the garage and cry. Just weep and weep. We set up the garage for him—made it a little workshop, had a bench and one of those old, spaceship-looking fridges out there, I don't know that you remember that. But back then even he'd say to me: don't ever come in my workshop. Even if I'm yelling or something, just leave me be. I knew enough to never ask him about it.

But when he'd be out there sometimes I'd sit just right on the other side of the door, like I was a dog or something. I don't know why I'd do it. Somehow I thought that having me there would make it better, would make whatever he was feeling be a bit less because I was there to somehow soften it. He never knew I was there, far as I know. Like I said, we didn't talk about it.

What was he upset about?

Who knows? she said. She started smoking then. The cigarette just appeared in her mouth, already lit.

But that's not really the point. The point was he never talked about it. What kind of shit is that? We weren't friends, you know, not like you and Val. I couldn't just walk in there and sit on the concrete and say I love you, I'm not leaving, go on and tell me all about it. It just wasn't like that.

Is Dad happy now?

Now? She shrugged. I haven't seen him. But I bet he is. He's been busy with what's her face, helping her clean that house and all. That keeps him moving.

What's her face was Susie, my stepmother. She was still alive.

The point is, she kept on, your father and I could never be more than one self. That's what made him hide like that out there. He could only be one self all the time: strong, stoic, family man, that sort of thing. He couldn't ever be weak, couldn't need me as an equal.

We were always only ever one person, no matter who we were with. I couldn't be the person I am here with you, and the person I was there at home. You couldn't have different sides. There just wasn't room for that kind of movement. And it'd make you damn well burst.

That's the hardest part about being dead. Realizing how much all the shit that kept you down in your life was bullshit. All anybody does when they first get here is go around saying why the hell didn't I ever do that? What was I thinking?

What you're thinking about doing—and I'm going to say it here, I know what you're thinking about doing, gassing all those people— that's not something that can be supported. It's not a way to grow, it's something that causes harm.

You can't, all right? She put her cigarette out and it disappeared. That's not how this works.

I could smell the Clove. How was that possible?

Don't do this thing. It's not going to go well.

Don't.

5

The day of the wedding rehearsal I figured I'd rehearse too, reviewing my notes and levels, testing my equipment. I put the mask on and walked around the house. Biscuit came downstairs and stopped, all fluffed. I stood still and we looked at each other.

You look pitiful, my mother said from the dining room. See, even that cat thinks so. Look at your owner, your big-hearted owner. What's the matter with you?

I pulled the mask off and stomped off into the kitchen.

Now you're mad?

You're not supposed to see this.

I know you think you've got your selves all nice and compartmentalized. The person you are for me isn't the person you are with all this nonsense. But guess what? I'm not going anywhere. Whatever you end up doing I'm going to be with you.

This isn't about you, Mom.

It was awful having her around. Every move I made I'd see her out the corner of my eye: having a stare down with Biscuit, matching my laundry socks by having them float together in the air, running around in the vacant lot next door, chasing squirrels.

At first I tried to hide what I was doing, sneaking the monitors out to my car and sliding them down in the front bench seat. I knew that she already knew what I was doing, but having her there made me feel worse about it. I'd waffle between guilt and shame and defiance. Who is she to tell me what to do? What does she know about how I'm feeling?

I spent the rest of the day trying to ignore her. I went to the Y and ran on the track, sat in the hot tub. Mom went and sat next to some kid who was having a bad day at swimming lessons. Just sat down next to him on the side of the pool. I couldn't tell if the kid saw her, but he started mimicking her. She'd splash her legs in the pool, he'd do the same. Fuck the deep end, she said. Fuck the deep end, the kid said back.

Val would go to the Y most every morning and do a different workout each time. Sometimes she'd swim, or do weights, or just walk for a while on the treadmill. But at the end, like clockwork, she'd be in the hot tub for "recovery."

Every night she'd tell me stories about the old ladies in the hot tub. They were all widows in their 80s, there for the morning water aerobics class. They love to bullshit, she'd say. And they're so real. When one of the women died, the rest talked about her upcoming funeral like was just part of a regular day.

"Well, so Betty's is at four today."

"Is it four?"

"Visiting starts at four. Should go until seven."

"Think they'll have sandwiches?"

"Oh, they'll have sandwiches. Betty was really clear with the funeral home on that. Don't you remember the day she went in and planned it? She told us all about it. 'Make sure he gets those Maid-Rite sandwiches for the wake, girls. I know they smell but I already paid for them.'"

I toweled off and got in the shower.

Mom was in the car waiting when I got out. I pulled the door shut behind me.

Why don't you just move away? she said. Move somewhere you and Val never were and start over. I'm not talking Prague or anything. Palo. Or Hiawatha. Or even just the other side of the Cedar River. You don't have to go far. Just a new start.

Then she'd really be gone, I said. Here I run into her all the time, but at least I run into her.

I don't think you can handle that right now.

I shook my head and put my forehead down on the steering wheel. I can't not run into her, Mom. If I'm going to stay down here, I can't not run into her.

When we got home I went upstairs and sat in my bedroom with

Biscuit, both of us on the bed, just looking out the window. I called Val. I called again and again, just listening to her message.

I'll call you back as soon as I can, she said.

6

It was Saturday, the day of the wedding, and I took the bus across town for breakfast and to leisurely make my way into the hotel. There was a conference for children's book illustrators that afternoon, as well as some robotics competition, so there'd be lots of activity. Plenty going on.

I didn't want to be in a hurry. I was that way about lots of things: travel, holiday shopping, even getting up in the morning. Start early and make the whole experience more pleasurable. Give yourself time to manage things that inevitably go wrong.

I expected my mother to come with me. But when I woke up she wasn't there. No trace of her. No smoke, no feeling, nothing. It was like she'd never been there at all.

I had been ready for a fight, a confrontation, something. To be turned loose on my own felt like cheating, like it was too easy.

Biscuit was hiding under the bed. No ceremony from her.

I took the 66A bus into the Westcott neighborhood, then ate breakfast alone at Mom's Café. I was a regular here. Keep doing the things you always do, I thought. Kathy put me in the tiny booth on the right-hand side, the one with all the pictures of old downtown drugstores. I looked at these photos every time I sat here, and every time I saw something new: a creepy kid peeking out from the backroom; a broom in the back corner; a sullen waitress who had forgotten her matching cap.

I texted Mark that I was over here and asked if he wanted me to check in on anything. Also not unusual.

If you want, he said. One of those illustrators is hot.

I walked the rest of the way, my gear nestled into my upscale leather bag, making me look like a fashionable walker, part of the neighborhood. This part of town was a blend of shops and houses and then the conference center, tucked back on a wooded lot. I followed Lancaster Avenue to the bike trail, then cut up through the woods, past where the employees took their smoke breaks.

No one was around as I made my way up the backstairs. I went around on the floor to see how the events were set: show my face, see if I could be useful.

I helped the folks at the registration desk get their computers set up and connected to the Wi-Fi, and showed them the fastest route to the bathrooms.

The robotics competition was in full swing, with middle school kids yelling like they were at a small-scale monster truck rally.

To the ballroom, I thought.

The hospitality staff had already set the tables and were close to having all the place settings in order. The head table was covered in overdone centerpieces.

"Those assholes make you come in?" Patrick, one of the staff, hollered at me. "Thought you didn't work summers."

"I was at Mom's for breakfast," I explained. "Mark asked me to just pop in, see if everything's okay."

"So far, so good," he said. "You may as well get out of here. Somebody always finds something for you to do around here."

I walked around the room, checking the cables, the laptop. I thumbed through their slide show—all the images were taken on their phones, then holding the phone out in front of them. People look so lonesome taking their own photos. Is there not a single other person around who could take your photo?

The crew started in then on the dance floor, locking it in place off to the side for an easy transition from dinner to dancing.

"Where's the gift table?" I asked. Joyce looked up from the install and nodded her head towards the side entrance.

I had my positions: where guests would enter, where they might congregate, and, thanks to checking the set list by the DJ booth, when the music would start.

Just before the cake, I thought. No one leaves before cake.

Val and I didn't have cake at our wedding. We got married in the middle of July out at the Little Brown Church in Nashua and packed a picnic. All of our guests packed a salad to share, and we brought roasted chicken we kept cold in our old cooler, as well as three pies, which was plenty for twenty people.

I brought a radio along for music, and Mark brought a few yard games for entertainment. It had been a beastly hot week, I remember, but that day was fine: with the wide oak trees and breeze, we were comfortable. I would look over at Val, again and again, and see her there with those big clouds rolling behind her, the deep blue sky, the grass valley behind that stretched down to Dry Run Creek.

She had a big, toothy grin, Val. And a habit of putting her hand on my shoulder when she made a point. I was taller than her, with wider shoulders, but she'd just meat her hand on my shoulder like she was about to climb up.

We had raspberry pie, a strawberry, and a rhubarb. The rhubarb went first. It was the first of the season, and everyone was ready for a taste.

Have I had rhubarb since? It's one of those flavors that if you think on it hard enough, you can nearly feel your mouth pucker: the smell of it, the stringy green-pinkness of it, the bite and the calm that comes from the sugar. I could smell it now.

I walked out into the empty staging area, took a clipboard, and threw it.

—

For all the things Val and I talked about—and we talked about a lot—we never had a conversation about end of life. What we wanted, how we wanted it, that sort of thing. Part of it might have come from never being able to shake those midwestern tendencies: it was so unheard of—and uncomfortable—to ask someone to do something lavish for you when you had no means of assisting. I wanted a funeral, but I wouldn't dream of mentioning it until I could afford to prepay it.

But what gets forgotten is that for us remaining, we'd love some direction. Love one last connection with the dead, one last project to do together. From casual conversations I knew Val was open to cremation—she had favorite parks, a favorite river in Wisconsin, a favorite constellation I could throw her towards—but she'd also mentioned being buried in Cedar Rapids.

In the end, I did what I wanted, and what I hoped she was okay with. I had her cremated and buried half of her ashes at Oak Shade Cemetery with a tall stone. The other half I took out to the Wapsipinicon, where she loved to float. I sprinkled some in my car, in the house, in the yard. I wanted to know she was all around me, always. And I liked knowing she was in the cemetery, too. That there was somewhere I could go to visit, bring her flowers.

Modern, and old fashioned. That was us.

I made a point of going back in the ballroom one last time and saying goodbye to Patrick, just so one person would see me leaving. "I'm out of here," I said, then joked: "You never saw me."

"That's right," he said. "I'll be out of here, too, as soon as I can."

I made my way out of the public area and into the guts of the building, popping the access panel from inside the back stairwell. Here the fine tile of the hotel gave way to cement floors and pools of water from condensation dripping off the boilers.

On the second landing I passed through another stairwell until I found the door to the pool chemical storage area. Now I was directly underneath the ballroom. I kept the lights off and turned on my headlamp.

The ventilation track leading up the ballroom ran through this room, and I climbed up and opened a passage. It made that slight, familiar echoing noise you hear when the system turns on or off. Expands and contracts.

It was a big room, the ballroom: 7,819 square feet. To have enough CO_2 in there to cause some illness, hopefully around five hundred parts per million, I'd have to get started early. I looked at my watch.

I'd be here for hours, I knew. Before disconnecting the venting tube for the pool heater, I unwrapped a candy bar and ate it, standing there in the dark. Then I got to work.

7

"Iowa ranks dead last for mental health care," gubernatorial candidate
Cody Nielsen railed at a campaign stop. "By opening up the state to sports betting we can then take that revenue and direct it towards mental health programming."

"So by encouraging gambling we'll have money to support addiction programs, such as gambling?" asked Dani Schneider, host of Iowa in Focus.

"Not just gambling addiction. All mental health issues."

"Sports betting is estimated to generate fifteen million dollars in state revenue," Schneider continued. "Last year alone the state granted seventy-seven million in tax credits to businesses. Rolling back just some of those credits would result in millions more available funds for mental health in the state. We wouldn't need to encourage people to gamble."

"Tax credits are complicated, Ms. Schneider. When I'm governor, we'll carefully consider all the options."

I didn't know it then, but my mother was waiting outside the pool maintenance door. She'd be standing, or sitting, or sometimes leaning up against the door. She didn't weigh anything, so I didn't hear a click or a shifting. But she was there just the same.

One of the last things Val and I did together was have dinner. I loved to cook, so I'd have food going every night. We ate late. I'd get home around 5:30 p.m. and we'd change clothes and sit in the living room and have cocktails. Talk about our days. Val loved meat and crackers, so I'd make a point of stocking up on sudzuk and svinjski vrat from the Bosnian market and we'd snack on that. Then I'd get started on dinner.

Sometimes she'd run the vacuum or putter around the house while I cooked, but other nights she'd sit at our little kitchen table and read me bits from the morning paper. We knew that other people didn't live like this anymore. But every night felt like vacation, like a holiday. Phones were off, the work day was finished, and we could just eat, and talk, and enjoy.

Val hated meeting with clients at night because it burst into this routine. That night I'd poured her a small vodka tonic, and loaded her up on meat, cheese, and crackers so she wouldn't get hungry in the middle of the session.

"Just call me when you're leaving," I said. "I'll start cooking and have it ready when you're home."

She had called. Said she'd make a quick stop at Menards and be on her way.

"Roasted chicken breast and potatoes okay?" I said. "Maybe a fruit salad?"

"Fruit-a-toot!" she said. "I love you, baby."

"Come on home. Love you."

I didn't worry when she was late. She knew everyone, and sometimes she got to talking with the boys at Menards. Or maybe the client called her back in for one more thing. But by eight I started to worry. I took her dinner out of the warming oven and put it in the fridge. I called.

"I'll call you back as soon as I can."

At nine I went out. I didn't know exactly where her client lived, just that she had to drive over to the northwest side. So I followed the main routes she usually took: down Independence, up 19th Street, up and down Lafayette. I'd left a note on the dining room table for her to call me, one on the fridge.

It was after ten and I didn't want to stop driving. My phone hadn't rung. If I stopped it would be like admitting something was wrong. And what if she was just around that corner? If her phone had died, if she was stuck someplace?

At midnight I called the station and reported her missing.

How many people had heard the crash? Who else could have called, could have stopped their car, walked outside of their goddamn house?

I put my gas mask on and carefully unfastened the exhaust for the pool heater, then redirected it into the air duct for the ballroom. It took ten minutes, tops, and that was with me taking my time. I stood back and looked at it, touched the pipe to make sure it was running. Then I sat on the floor, on my bag, my levels in my lap. I set an alarm for three hours. Then I turned on my flashlight and started working on the day's crossword.

The part I hadn't thought of—well, that I hadn't figured out a solution for—was how to tell the level of CO2 in the ballroom without going into the ballroom. I couldn't figure out a way to remote in, or set up a remote sensor, and I didn't want to leave and come back, leave and come back. Too many variables, too many people to see me. This was the only point left to chance.

Either people would get sick, or they wouldn't, I thought. I'd either let enough in, or not enough.

At the end of the night, I'd close up the duct work to the ballroom, and set the pool heater vent slightly off, like it just slipped out of its case. I'd turn off the pilot light. A cold pool would alert staff to check the heater, and they'd see the venting, raise the alarm about CO2 buildup, and everything would be ventilated.

There was an exit right out this stairwell. I'd walk down the hill to the bike trail and wind up back on Lancaster, where I'd catch the bus for home.

A steady plan.

Boy, it's dark in here.

"As we said earlier, if you are having suicidal thoughts, please call the suicide hotline at 988. We're encouraging people to write this number down and keep it in your wallet in case you, or someone you know, needs it in the future."

I dozed off then, just for a minute. I had a dream that I was somewhere—it was all hazy—and a few other people were there. I couldn't see their faces, but I could tell they were there. Everything was so distant, it was like we were underwater: the sounds, the movement of the shapes. I knew the people; there was a comfortable, old feeling being there. I was younger, somehow. I was safe. People were laughing. There was the feeling of being held without being touched.

For a while after Val was gone, I didn't cook at all. I reverted back to my feral days and just ate cereal, standing up in the kitchen. The Bosnian meats got pushed to the back of the refrigerator. I didn't pour out the liquor, but watched the bottles get dusty, watched Val's vodka get covered in a fine layer of ice from the freezer.

I ate out more. I gained weight, not in once place, but just sort of all over. I looked softer, a little swollen, my eyes not as bright, my rings too tight.

Days would just bleed into the next. Everything was boring. I'd think about trying a new recipe, or going to the Y, just doing something different and possibly good for myself. But then I'd think how it really didn't matter, how one day, one meal, wouldn't make a difference, and I'd keep on down my same slide.

When I woke up it was after six. The reception started at four. My levels said it was 900 ppm in the storage room, a deadly level, and that was with me putting the exhaust pipe directly into the duct work. Was that enough to fill the ballroom?

It's enough to fill the pool room, I'll tell you that, my mother said. She was there, in the room with me. She gestured to the west wall. Think all that gas just stays in here? It's been seeping through all afternoon.

Is there anybody in there?

Just a birthday party, my mother shrugged. A pack of boys.

I jumped back on top of the heater and took the pool exhaust out of the ductwork. I resealed the ducts, then left the exhaust pipe slightly out of its venting, like I planned. A perfect accident.

I grabbed all my gear, tucked it in my bag, and ran out the door into the stairwell. I pushed the door into the hotel hallway and pulled the fire alarm.

—

My nephew wouldn't get a tiny house, but something more practical: a tear-drop trailer. That way he could set it up at a camp and drive into town for supplies. It weighed nothing, and he could tow it himself. He traveled the country for two years with that thing: parking at camps, picking up work here and there as a camp host.

His girlfriend tried to talk him out of it. People will do that, I said to him. People who are jealous.

It's easy to be on the fence about kids. To not want to push one out, not really (maybe?), but I'd been open to it. Thought about how a child's feet would sound pounding down the stairs, how their face would flush from sitting on the old cast iron heating grate. I had wanted boys. Sinewy rails of boys, built like their mother.

They would swim, and burn, and holler to one another. Tackle and jump like puppies, like overeager golden retrievers. The bags of Chex Mix and Chicken in a Biskit would be soggy at the end of the party. The towels thick with humidity. Their feet rubbed raw from running, then jumping, then rocking back and forth on the pool deck.

I would wait outside to collect them, the car running. And out they would come, bare-chested, unselfconscious, hair akimbo, mouths open, the youngest with teeth still missing. Hungry and wet and loud loud loud.

—

The pool was empty except for my mother, collapsed in her track suit between the hot tub and the pool. I dashed in.

Mom, what the hell? I said.

Open that emergency door to the deck, she said. Drag me out there.

I couldn't touch her, because there was nothing to touch. My hands didn't go through her, but stopped just an inch or so above her. There was no moving closer; it was like I hit something pliable. Like she was encased in a grabbable film.

I dragged her out, then stood there over her, catching my breath.

Take that mask off, she said. And don't go back in there. You'll kill yourself.

Are you dying? I said.

Duh, she smiled. Go on. Go.

I ran around the outside of the building and down the hill to the parking lot. My bag looped securely over me, my mask buckled in tight. From here I made my way up to the main desk.

Jimmy, the manager, a friend of ours, was at the front. I told him what happened. Or what I thought had happened. Or what I said had happened.

Shit, he said. Anybody in there?

One woman, I said. An old lady in a tracksuit.

He raised an eyebrow. Is she dead?

I don't think so, I said.

I didn't know how to swim. Or how to do CPR. Or French braid hair, build a retaining wall, paint a picture.

What I could do was wash and dress a wound. Give a proper handshake. Iron a shirt. Trap an animal. Refinish a floor, sanding over and over again, like that French painting. Toiling slowly, focusing on the grooves, the stubborn dark spots, instead instead instead…

There were plenty of people around, then. Plenty to do. The firefighters arrived just as soon as I talked with Jimmy. They'd driven their gleaming trucks out of the Westcott station and were focused, alert, calm, as they laid on the horn, loud, loud, loud, to stop traffic, to get through the intersection. Two trucks to the back, two to the front.

Jimmy directed them (his nametag: James) to the pool area. No fire, he said. I don't think. We think it's gas.

The firefighters barked at each other, moved their arms wide.

Some upstairs, some to the back. Everybody out, everybody out.

Jimmy and I stood across 17th street. The police blocked traffic for two blocks, directing people down Westcott. A firefighter came over to Jimmy and told him what they'd found: the venting for the pool heater had slipped, and CO_2 poured out into the pool and up into the ballroom: 600 ppm. I'd done it.

"We're still checking rooms to see if anyone else needs assistance. We're evaluating the guests from that wedding, see if anybody's got a headache or anything."

"What about that woman at the pool?" Jimmy asked.

The man shook his head. "We asked if she wanted treatment, but she wouldn't let anybody near her. We let her be for a minute, see if she'd come around, but then next we knew she was gone." He shrugged.

"Some people are like that. She mighta broken in and was afraid she'd get in trouble."

The firefighter, the chief I would learn, turned and shook my hand. "You're a hero. This could have been much, much worse."

"Oh, no," I said.

"You are. You're a hero, my friend."

It became a feel-good story. Twenty-three guests from the wedding reception were taken to St. Anthony's Hospital, but no one died. Jimmy moved the reception to Sartori Park, called in a favor to a friend in Collateral, a huge local band, and they agreed to play for free. He was smart, Jimmy. Turning this all into good press.

In the pictures in the paper, the guests look exuberant. A hot, summer night, dancing by the trees, the bride and groom together, leaning on one another, touching, the entire night.

There were no terrible decorations. No meat dishes. No mega-expensive custom dance floor.

I'd be stupid to think one night could change things. That one night could make this couple, this party, all of us, focus; that one moment could untether us, direct us to the things and people that matter.

But something shifted for me. Something broke loose then, and fell away.

I was five miles from home. Five miles back down the bike trail, which eventually spit out onto Central, which turned into Ellen Street. With traffic being blocked off, I knew the buses would be rerouted, delayed, pushed back.

Time shifts on a long walk like that, a walk you've never done. When I got within two miles, I felt like I was in the homestretch. At one mile, I thought: this is nothing. I've got this. I'll be back in no time.

By the time I made it home it was getting dark. Biscuit was hungry and sitting in the window. My back steps were littered in Clove cigarette butts. I knew I wouldn't see my mother again, not like I had. I left the butts where they were.

I went upstairs and fed the cat, then took my journal and sat inside Val's closet.

It was just like she'd left it: half the clothes on hangers, the other half piled on the floor. An unrolled sleeping bag was in the mix, along with boots, her old prom dress, and some pillows from childhood she couldn't get rid of, that I might never get rid of.

It was the only place in the house that still smelled like her. I closed the door behind me to preserve it.

In the dim closet light, I took out my journal and started to read.

Quite a story.

Grief will grab you. It'll hit you in different ways.

I went outside then. I went for a long walk, past Donutland and Collins Road, all the way downtown. A house between 28th and 29th Street had a huge cage in the front yard with a bunny in it. Everything likes time outside.

When I got home, Biscuit ate out of my hand for the first time.

Each day gets a little better.

DIRECT CONNECTION

THEN

A Lesson in Geography

When things were quiet at the bookstore Michael liked to think about where his wife could be: down the street at Jack and Jill, haggling over the price of hamburger; sitting on the porch, darning socks. If he focused hard he could see her moving, picture her clothes. Sometimes, though not lately, he could remember what she smelled like.

Route walked through the shop door, a small bell announcing her arrival.

"Papa!" she bellowed, dropping her book bag in front of his desk. She was his daughter—red haired and slender—but her manner was all Rita. Route extended her hands and took a small bow. "I've arrived!" She was seven.

Michael had worked at Tremont Street for ten years. The store wasn't on Tremont—it was on 22nd—but the owner lived on Tremont and wasn't terribly creative. The name made it confusing for giving directions. Someone would call the store: "No, the store's named Tremont Street, but we're located on College and 22nd. That's correct, not Tremont." But the owner, Pete, Michael's boss, refused to change it. When Michael placed their ad in the Yellow

Pages, he included a little map. One night after work, he walked the three blocks to the corner of 22nd and Tremont and nailed a sign to the telephone pole. It read: "Books: Three blocks." He drew a large, red arrow pointing west.

Route went and visited with the college kids at the coffee bar and, like every day, they took her after-school snack out of the staff fridge and put her carrots, apple slices and peanut butter on a plate, like it had been for purchase. She balanced the food on one hand as though she were serving cocktails.

"How was it today?" Michael asked.

Route shrugged and ate a slice of apple. She didn't say anything. She always had plenty to say.

"You just want to read for a bit?"

She nodded and settled into a beanbag.

A few college kids came in and browsed. An elderly couple brought up a stack of mysteries to purchase. But mostly Michael did what he did every afternoon at this time. Sorted new books for the stacks. Ran the sweeper. Emptied the trash. Chris Isaak played on his small cassette player.

At five he and Route walked the two blocks home. Michael opened and closed his hand, and Route put her hand in his. It was an old game between them, and he dreaded the day she felt too old for it.

"A retired professor brought in forty-three old geography books today," Michael said.

"What's geography?"

"It's maps. And places. The study of places and people and how they live."

"Oh."

"But it changes all the time. People change, countries change, so these books, none of them are any good or much use to people."

"Lindsay was mean to me," Route said.

This was it then, he thought.

"Oh?" he said

"She said in front of everyone on the playground that I don't have a TV. Then she said I was a weirdo."

"What's wrong with not having a television?"

"All the kids have them."

Michael knew this. He knew that it was unusual not to have a television. Years ago, when Pete found out Michael and his wife didn't have one, he was shocked. Michael came to work the next day and a ten-inch, black-and-white set was sitting on his desk.

"I had an extra," Pete said.

Michael took it home to be nice. He and Rita put it in the back of the closet and he hadn't thought about it since.

"So you want a television because the other kids have one?"

Route shrugged. "I don't know."

They stood in front of their towering old house and Michael shoved the main door open with his hip. It was never locked. Inside, Michael could smell food from the other apartments as he climbed the worn staircase. He mentally went through what he had in the kitchen, thinking about what he could make quickly.

"I'm sorry if she made you feel bad." He made sure to look her full in the face when he said this. "You are not a weirdo. You're a wonderful girl."

"Why don't we have a television?" Route asked, standing outside their apartment door. "Are they expensive?"

Michael was not a church man but he was a man of faith. And he believed the Lord did not create him to be idle. Man was created to do work, good work; there was satisfaction in a job well done, and that satisfaction, that sense of order and purpose, did not come from watching sitcoms on television.

He felt a wave of longing wash over him. He held on to the knob of the apartment door, hoping Rita would be inside. That she'd be sitting at the counter, shelling peanuts. That the two of them could walk down the hall and talk about this. Talk about what was the right thing to do.

He opened the door, but everything was just as he had left it.

The apartment wasn't so much an apartment as it was one good sized room. There was a thin rug on the floor and a mattress laid right down on it. There was a coffee table and a very small kitchen, divided from the rest of the space by a counter, where they sat for their meals. When Route was small, he, his wife, and Route all shared the double bed. But now that Route was getting older, Michael knew she was going to need some space of her own. So in the evenings he rolled out a sleeping bag on the kitchen floor and slept behind the counter to give her some privacy.

The walls were lined with bookshelves filled with castoffs from the book store. Above the stacks were pictures drawn by Route, all taped or tacked to the walls. As Michael cooked and listened to KUNI, Route did her schoolwork at the coffee table. Spelling lists, handwriting exercises, reading. She was just finished with her math exercises when Michael dished up some stir-fry. She had her own set of chopsticks.

—

Rita had been a smoker for years, they both had been, and when she started complaining of chest pains neither of them thought much of it. She smoked. Of course she'd be out of breath when she got to the top of the stairs. And neither of them thought much of it when she started going to bed earlier, when she started eating less and less of her dinner. They were getting older. Bodies and appetites changed. Wasn't this just the way things went?

He thought about those moments every day, at the oddest times. When he was cutting up vegetables, or watering her old spider plants, the plants he hated but couldn't bring himself to throw away. Why didn't he notice? Why didn't he do something sooner?

It happened on a Tuesday morning. Route was up and dressed and eating her breakfast and Rita was still in bed. Michael tried to wake her but she didn't feel right. Her skin was cold, clammy. She opened up her eyes and said she just wanted some more sleep. Just to let her sleep.

It wasn't two weeks and she was gone. Route was four.

"Why do you do that?" Route asked, watching her father adjust the antenna. She had only seen color sets, he realized: sets hooked up to cable. A black and white picture was not something that belonged in her world. As the picture slowly began to take shape, Michael felt a churning in the pit of his stomach. It didn't feel right having a set, even an old one, here in the house, but it also didn't feel right to keep his daughter sheltered from the world. Suddenly there was the sound of people talking and then, when the picture disappeared, the deafening noise of static. Route put her hands over her ears.

"It's like a radio. It comes through the air." Michael stopped what he was doing and pulled a book off the shelf. He opened it to a picture of a television.

"See?"

Route looked at the diagram, studying the book while her father made more adjustments.

When the picture came in clearly, Route clapped her hands and pulled her knees to her chest.

"*The Cosby Show!*" she squealed. "Papa, watch!"

Michael walked down the hall to use the bathroom. There were two rooms, two doors off the hallway. One for the stool, another for the tub and shower. Sometimes, if the stool was occupied and he was desperate, he was known to pee in the tub. But this wasn't something he told Route about. He didn't want to encourage her.

"Rita, I don't like it," he said. He closed the door. This was the only space in the world he had to himself, and it wasn't his. "I don't like her watching that television, but I want her to know what it is. That seemed important right then. I hope you can forgive me."

When he spoke to her, he could feel her response come to him in waves. It was a warm sensation in his head. Even when she was alive, he could feel her talking to him in this way. When he was lonesome or in need, it was as if he could channel her. They never talked about it, the way they had with each other. But he knew.

The world is changing, he could hear her say. *I'm sorry I'm not there with you. I know this is hard for you.*

"Is this the right thing to do? I just don't know, Rita," he said. He spoke out loud, like she was right there next to him. "She needs to know about the world. She needs to read and go outside, not look at some box. She can't be idle. Being idle would hurt her."

Give her the options. She'll make her own choices, Rita said. *If you don't give her options, she'll resent you.*

"I miss you something crazy," he said, looking at himself in the mirror. He expected to see her there behind him, her hair huge in the humidity.

Just love her, she said. *Just love her something fierce.*

Before he walked back in to the apartment, Michael could hear Route changing the channels, the loud thump of the knob turning.

"There are only three pictures," she said.

"That's right."

"You can't make more?"

Michael shook his head. "But you can pick out any book you want for before bed. We got to get you tucked in. What book do you want?"

She stood up and looked at one, then slowly moved to another, like she was looking at works in the museum. Michael noticed then that she was getting taller. *Rita*, he thought. *She's getting taller. She'll be a woman and gone before I know it.*

"Do we have a geography book?"

"If you get ready for bed, I'll find you one."

Route grabbed her bathroom case. She kept her bedroom slippers by the door and Michael could hear her shuffling loudly down the hall.

He turned the television off, and felt a wave of relief wash over him.

Thank you, Rita, he said in his head. *Thank you for this. For Route, for her making good decisions.*

Don't pray to me, he could hear her respond. *Pray to Mary, to the*

Lord. Thank them.

Atlases didn't sell well at the store, so Michael had a few in the apartment to choose from. He laid the largest out on the bed, open to the world. Route bounced back into the room, her hair damp.

"Sit up here," he said, getting out a hairbrush.

She stuck her tongue out and picked up the book.

The continents were easy. She had heard of those before. But the smaller countries were something new.

"Even these little dots? These are whole countries?" She pointed to Indonesia, the Solomon Islands. "What's here?" she pointed.

"That's Vanuatu."

"Vanuatu." She paused. "It's so tiny!"

"You know how we can walk a little ways and see corn? For miles and miles? In Vanuatu people walk a little bit and they see the ocean."

He could tell that didn't mean much to Route. The only body of water she had ever seen was the Cedar River.

"You know how much farm land there is? Think of all the corn we have. Now imagine if it was all water."

"All of it?"

"Yes. That's what an island is like. Take away the corn and put water in its place."

She paused for a minute. "All the way to Traer?"

"Traer, Waverly, Charles City—all of it. If all of that in-between was water." He pointed to the Tasman Sea, the South Pacific. "Everywhere there's blue, that's water."

"But you just said all those towns, Papa. People can't live in the water."

He got up then and put the book under his arm.

"I'm not being very helpful," he said. "Let's put your slippers on."

Off the front of the house was a porch. Over the years the neighbors arranged a collection of found furniture, from single dining room chairs to metal stools. Once a year Michael came out and pitched the broken and the derelict pieces, and more seats always came to take their place.

The sun was setting earlier, a sign on the coming winter. But the nights were still warm. The street outside was quiet, the only sound coming from the occasional car passing, red lights flickering at the approaching stop sign.

Michael pulled two chairs up and put their backs against the railing. He sat down and motioned from Route to do the same.

"Lean way back," he said. "Just your head. You stay put here in the chair."

They both leaned their heads back on the railing, looking up at the clear night sky. Michael took a deep breath. This was what he had done on dates with Rita, what they did on the roof of their first apartment. When the thought of Rita, really thought of her, he worried he would be physically sick, he missed her that much.

"Pick a star and look at it. That's like Vanuatu. You see that there? It's all contained in one spot, and the sky around it is water. If you wanted to get from one star to the next, you'd just take a little boat."

He looked over at her staring at the clear night sky. Route would see the ocean in her lifetime. She would grow and travel and marry a woman and leave Iowa, her father, all this behind.

But when Michael would think of her, years later, as he worked up the courage to write her a letter, he would picture her there on the porch beside him the night she discovered islands. Route, the girl, the daughter he loved, pointing her finger up to the sky.

Route turned eight. She turned nine.

When Route was ten, Michael bought her a bike—with gears—for her birthday and she took to riding it for hours at a time. Michael gave her boundaries: Hudson Road to the west, 18th Street to the north, Ellis Boulevard east and University Avenue south. A square mile. She would get up early on Saturday mornings and go to the corner of 18th and Ellis to look at the signs posted for garage sales. She kept a small notebook in her pocket and scribbled down addresses, then spent the rest of the morning darting from one sale to the next, spending her allowance on jewelry, books, and sometimes old art prints that she and Michael would hang in the hallway for everyone to see.

When she was out riding Michael spread the paper out on the coffee table and looked at the ads for apartments. It was time, he knew. Route was getting older, and the apartment was getting smaller and smaller. But Michael worried about having an apartment that was completely self-contained. How would Route know her neighbors? Would it just be the two of them, sealed away in some small box with no one to talk to?

Finally, after weeks of searching, a furnished one-bedroom apartment opened up in the small brick apartment complex down the hill, about six blocks from their current place. He could still walk to work at the bookstore, use the same grocery store. Route could take the bedroom while he slept on the couch. There was a private bath and, most importantly for Michael, a shared kitchen and dining area with two other apartments. He signed the paperwork that day.

"It's so big!" Route said when he took her to see it. She spun around the living room, then ran into the bedroom. "And this whole room is mine? Papa, really?" She raced from one end of the room to the other, then lay on the floor and pretended to make snow angels. She sat up suddenly. "Are we rich?"

While Route loved the apartment—loved taking long showers in their own bathroom, loved watching *Where in the World is Carmen Sandiego* as part of her weekly allotment of TV—Michael laid awake on the couch night after night. He struggled to make it through his shifts at the bookstore. On his lunch break he would walk home and try to nap, but he just lay there on the couch like he did every evening, staring up at the ceiling, wide awake.

Rita, he'd say. *Where'd you go?*

In the evenings Route liked to do her homework in the shared kitchen and talk with some of the other children in the building. One night Michael found her with a new family, a mother and daughter, playing a card game at the large table.

"Hello," Michael said, nodding at the woman. She wore her dark hair pulled back severely and her face looked both hardened and childlike at the same time. It was difficult to tell her age. Her brown eyes were piercing. She nodded at him, but didn't say anything.

"I'm Michael, Route's father."

The woman smiled and nodded again. She pointed to a young girl. The child put her cards down and gave Michael a big, toothy smile.

"I'm Nina. And that's my mama. Her name is Dijana. She doesn't speak much English yet."

"They're from Bosnia," Route said proudly. "I know where that is! Near the Adriatic Sea. Sit down, Papa. Play with us."

Michael sat across from Dijana and watched as she dealt cards three at a time, then two.

Nina explained the rules. Michael and Route would be partners, bidding for tricks. The game was strikingly similar to Euchre, and Michael caught on quickly.

When Nina took a trick, Dijana smiled and clapped her hands.

"We haven't had anyone to play with in a long time," Nina said, shuffling the cards. "My mom's very happy."

When the game finished, Dijana got up and started cooking.

"Route, are you getting hungry?" Michael asked. She nodded, not really listening. She was teaching Nina how to play Go Fish.

He rummaged through their cupboard and started cooking black beans and rice. Dijana took over the small countertop and rolled out some dough that had been sitting in the fridge. As she cooked, the smell was overwhelming.

Michael pointed at her dish and smiled. She nodded and smiled back.

"Your friends are nice," Michael said that night as Route got ready for bed.

"Nina's going to be in my grade," Route said, spitting out her toothpaste. "Can we walk to school together?"

"Sure."

"They used to live in Utica, in New York? I looked it up and can show you. That's how Nina learned English. Now they live here so her mom can work at Rath. Are there books about the war? Papa, there are terrible things happening there. Nina's dad died and they had to move all the way over here to get away."

"It's in the papers. I can bring you papers home."

Route smiled. She tied her hair back to wash her face. Her hair was long and straight and red. It was beautiful.

"Want to know how to say 'Hello?' *Zdravo*."

Route made a list of common phrases and taped it to their bathroom mirror. Every morning and every night Michael would see these phrases, hear Dijana's voice in his head. *Hello, goodbye. How are you?* Michael also had Route write down the numbers and translations for Jack, King, Queen and Ace. As he brushed his teeth, Michael repeated the words over and over in his head. And he thought about Dijana. He wondered what she missed most about her city, what it was like to live through the war. What did she look like with her hair down?

Soon Michael and Route fell into a routine and ate dinner and played cards with Nina and Dijana every night. At first Dijana didn't like the idea of Michael cooking, but his food was good and soon she became comfortable with him taking care of dinner a few nights a week. The girls did their homework together at the table while they cleaned up, and Michael was amazed at how Route was learning to switch back and forth between English and Bosnian.

When she made a mistake, she and Nina would erupt in peals of laughter. Sometimes Michael would stop drying dishes and stand back in awe of how happy his daughter was, happier than he ever imagined she could be with Rita gone.

On Sunday nights, Route started watching *60 Minutes* with Michael to try and learn more about the war. And during the week Michael started spending part of his mornings sorting through the children's books, looking for anything that might be of use to Dijana. Digging through the shelves, he found a beautifully illustrated children's dictionary, with clear definitions and pronunciations. It was perfect. As he counted out the change to pay for it, Michael found that his hands were shaking.

When he brought the books to their apartment, Dijana shook her head. When Michael insisted, she raced down the hall to the kitchen. He turned imploringly to Nina: "Tell her the books are free," he lied. "I don't have to pay for them."

"We must thank you. Please, let Mama make you something."

By the time Michael walked down the hall to the kitchen, Dijana had a bowlful of dough and was carefully brushing about thirty small tins with butter. Michael put the kettle on for tea, then poured two cups and sat down at the kitchen table. The sun had gone down but the curtains were still open, letting in the pale yellow light from the streetlamps. Dijana laid the tins on a cookie sheet, then put everything in the oven. Michael watched her as she meticulously cleaned her utensils and scrubbed the counter. He knew he was staring. When she turned to him, he smiled; she smiled back, then quickly returned to her cleaning.

When the cookies were done, Dijana sat down and put the

plate between them. Michael opened the children's dictionary and pointed at the pictures, saying the English word out loud. Dijana would repeat the word, then say the Bosnain word for the same object. They sat there together, looking at pictures, eating buttery nut cookies, until they realized they had eaten all the cookies on the plate.

Dijana started to laugh, and Michael smiled. She rubbed her belly.

"Hvala," he said, gesturing to the empty plate.

"Thank you," she said, collecting the books.

That night Michael stood in the bathroom and looked in the mirror. "Rita," he said. "You've been gone a long time, and I think there's someone I'd like to see." He paused then, waiting for a response. That feeling of warmth, that rush of connection. "Rita, she's beautiful. She's kind and loving. But I'm so scared. Rita, can you hear me? Where are you?" There was no response. Not a feeling, not a voice. He wanted Rita to be angry. He wanted her to come screaming back to him. But instead there was silence. He could feel a pit in his stomach opening up.

He went in and sat on Route's bed. He shook her leg lightly. There was a map of Bosnia over her head, with different cities circled in crayon.

"Papa?" she said sleepily. "What is it?"

"Do you remember your mother?" he said. He was holding a small stack of photos. "I miss your mother. Do you remember your mother?"

"What's the matter?" she tried to sit up. She pushed the covers off of her. "Papa, it's nighttime."

He never wanted to tell Route any of this. Never wanted her to be his confidant. It's important for the parents to be parents, he and Rita always said. But he sat there next to her, blindly showing her photos while he cried.

Route couldn't remember her father crying, couldn't remember him ever depending on her for anything. She got out of bed and sat next to him, taking the photos from him one by one. When he finished going through the stack, she handed them back to him.

"Stay right here," she said. "Right here, okay?"

A moment later she came back with Nina and Dijana, all dressed in pajamas and slippers. Route turned on her bedside lamp, filling the room with soft light. She didn't know what else to do, besides alert another adult.

Dijana sat on the bed a good distance away from Michael. She passed him a photo of her own, of her and her husband. She pointed to her husband and spoke softly in Bosnian, her voice rising and falling.

"I'm so scared," Michael said.

Dijana responded in Bosnian. He didn't know what she was saying, but he knew it was something similar. He took her hand and squeezed it. She squeezed back, hard. The girls sat on the floor in their nightgowns and held each other, watching, waiting to see what happened next.

Freedom

The day my girlfriend Shenandoah went missing, Andrew and I'd started drinking early. It was raining—hot, summer rain—and Andrew and I put together some homemade rain gear and trudged our way to Hy-Vee to get beer. By the time Shan got home for her lunch break we were laid out on the couches, ready to take naps for the rest of the afternoon. Plus, it was still raining. It was like the outside world was encouraging our behavior.

"Look at you," Shan said to me. "Are you naked?"

"No," I said, rustling around. "There are shorts on."

"It's not even noon." She shook her head. But she was laughing. My girl. "I haven't even eaten yet."

"Are you hungry?" Andrew asked. Shan sat down next to me on the sofa. She touched my arm, I remember. "We went to the store," Andrew finished.

"It's a rain suit," I explained.

"You wrapped yourself in an old plastic tarp."

"This is a garbage sack," Andrew declared, standing to model. "I just put holes in it."

Andrew was my oldest friend, a tall man who was up for anything.

We grew up playing ball in the middle of C Ave, just a few streets over from where I lived now. He was the guy who would come over at seven in the morning, or two in the morning, if you said you needed him or promised it would be fun.

"Okay, Chief." He called everybody *Chief*. "Give me two shakes."

Before Shan went missing, there was more going my way than ever before. Now, afterwards, I know it with this sense of hyper-awareness that makes me wish I could go back. Not because I could change anything, but just so I could pay attention.

Andrew turned on the television. Shan ate a sandwich, then she snuggled in next to me. She wiped water off me with a blanket.

"Can I borrow your car?"

"But you're warm."

"Where are your keys?"

"Sure," I said.

"Mine's shaking still. I just want to make sure I get back."

I got the keys and walked her out back. Our cars were parked side by side in the backyard, looking cleaner and shinier than ever.

"Home at three?" I asked.

Shan smiled.

I gave her my keys and she got in. I was still pretty drunk at this point, but I remember she didn't answer me, not really. She got in and put her seat belt on. It divided her breasts nicely and I looked for a while. She saw me looking and put her third finger on her chest. She didn't look sad or anything; she just looked like herself. But that was it.

"Okay, I gotta go," she said. "C'mere." She tilted her face towards me.

After she drove off, I got in her car and curled up in the backseat. It just seemed like the thing to do. I lay there listening to the rain on the roof. I remember thinking how nice it would have been if Shan didn't have to go back to work, if we could have just stayed together on the couch all afternoon. But Shan was practical. She was never late for work. She paid her bills, got up at the same time every morning. When she prayed at night—because she did—she mostly offered up prayers of thanksgiving. I'd never met someone like Shan: that grounded, that sure. That's why I never would have seen it coming.

When I got back inside Andrew and some stranger he knew were listening to old rap albums and smoking pot. I joined in. The man had brought more beer and we drank that too.

Other people might be working, I thought, *but it's our day off. We should do what we want.*

We sat there until it got close to dinner. Then the man went home and I remembered my legs, still wrapped in plastic.

"Good idea," Andrew said as I started cutting them out with a scissors. "Want me to do your other leg?"

"With what?" I only had one pair of scissors.

Andrew went into the kitchen and came back with a small knife.

"No," I said.

"It's serrated. It won't hurt. I'll keep the blade up."

"No."

"Jeez," he said, sitting back down on the sofa. "I'm just trying to help."

It was then that we started talking about Shenandoah. We noticed she wasn't home when she said she would be, but now that it was after five we put it in words and let it come out of our mouths. Now her absence was loose and in the room with us. It didn't feel good.

Shan and I had been dating for three years and had been living together for two. It had been a long time. I wanted to have a commitment ceremony, but she told me to wait. Her last relationship was good for a while, then it got real bad.

"I just want to enjoy this," she said. "I want to make sure we're sure."

"That you're sure," I said.

"We're sure," she emphasized.

So sometimes we were good and had Andrew and his date of the week over for dinner and cards, and sometimes I did dumb stuff like wrap myself in plastic and walk to Hy-Vee in the rain. But even when Shan and I were fighting, even when we had our moments, she always came home after work.

At six I started making calls. I called her work, her friends. At seven I called her folks. Andrew got up and put a frozen pizza in the oven. He handed me slices while I kept making calls. At eight I called the police, who said they couldn't do anything until more time passed.

"She's in my car," I said. "Does that help?"

"Do you want to report a stolen vehicle?"

"Can you look for that right away?"

"Yes. What kind of vehicle is it?"

—

When I got off the phone with the police I called more people: friends, family. I went through Shan's address book and started with the people who lived closest to us, then moved further out until I was sending messages all across northeast Iowa, up to parts of Minnesota. If someone didn't answer I repeated their number over and over again in my head and tried to picture the person in my mind. It calmed me. It made me think there were lots of people out there, all looking for Shan, all together on this rainy night.

At midnight Andrew said, "All right. We got to get out of the house."

"But she might call."

"If she does, she'll call back. Hell, people are going to be calling all night."

"Where are we going?"

"Do you have her keys?" Andrew didn't have a car but he was a much better driver than me. He was careful. And right then, wearing that garbage sack shirt, he was surprisingly rational.

Shan's car looked like it always did: Z1029 bumper stickers, clean floor mats, alphabetized music collection. I opened the glove box. I looked through her cassettes. I don't know what I was looking for—a clue, something—but I didn't find it.

"We're gonna drive her route. Just look for your car, or her, or anything. She got a flashlight in there?"

She did, of course. Whenever I needed something she had it. There was sunscreen in her glove box. Matches. A deck of cards. How could she be lost? How could she not be prepared for something?

—

We drove down 1st Avenue, into the belly of Cedar Rapids, past Guns and Gold Pawn, Caboose Stop Hobbies, the Casey's. There was a car in the Little Gem diner parking lot with a flat tire and a black garbage bag taped over the back-passenger window. The bag rustled in the breeze.

We pulled over. For a while there Shan and I went to Little Gem every Sunday night. An old woman with long grey hair, Dorothy, would wait on us and I was hoping she was on tonight. She knew us.

Dorothy stopped cleaning the counter when we walked in. She called me by name. I introduced her to Andrew, who apologized for wearing a garbage sack shirt.

I told Dorothy everything. We'd never had a personal conversation before but suddenly I felt very close to her. I told her about Shan's routine, about how long she'd been missing.

"I'm sorry, Hon, I haven't seen her. She stopped by a couple of times last week, but not today. I'm real sorry."

"What's she look like?" A man got up from his booth and came over. I showed him a picture from my wallet, one I took at a barbeque. Shan hated the picture because she thought she looked greasy, but I thought it was perfect. She was my everyday beauty.

"Nice-looking girl. You could put it up on the bulletin board with your number."

"Have you seen her?"

The man shook his head. He called his friends over and they looked. There was a whole group of us now, crowded around Dorothy. I wanted to take them all out with us; I wanted to invite them all over for a party. They carefully passed Shan's picture back and forth, trying not to leave fingerprints.

Dorothy gave me a piece of paper and some thumbtacks. It was strange leaving the picture behind, but Dorothy told me there'd be people in and out all night. I'd be sure to get calls.

"Write about your car, too," she said. "Put that all down."

"We'll say a prayer for her," one of the men said. Andrew shook his hand.

We stopped at every open business between home and work, talking to whoever was around. I didn't have another picture of Shan, so Andrew drew her face on the back of receipts, on napkins. At the Sip 'N' Stir they let him draw her face in pen on the wall behind the bar.

"This way people'll see her," the bartender said.

Andrew made more sketches on whatever paper people had in their pockets. It was amazing, the way he could pull Shan out of paystubs, matchbooks, to-do lists. It just took a few lines and there she was: her eyes, her hair, like that's where she'd been hiding all along.

When we got outside it had stopped raining. Andrew and I got back in the car and went past the railroad tracks, the lake, the Quaker plant that stood like a beacon in a cloud of oat-smelling fog.

"Becca went missing one time, you remember her? My old downstairs neighbor?" Andrew looked over at me. He was trying.

"Shan isn't Becca," I said.

"She was gone for like two days." Andrew pulled onto 380 and fired through the S curve. It was the middle of the night, and we were the only ones on the road. "We called the cops, her family, the whole bit, and turns out she was just over at Tony's on a bender. She was across the street the whole time."

"You think Shan's just out drinking."

"Didn't I tell you this story? Tony was that guy who always wore overalls."

"She's not across some street. Something's—"

"Hang on," Andrew said. "Hang on."

We pulled out of the bend and there was an eighteen-wheeler stopped right in the middle of the lane. Andrew parked on the shoulder and a man came running over to us, his eyes wild.

"He jumped. The kid just jumped in front of me. You gotta help him."

I'd seen dead people before, at funerals and in hospitals, but never out in the world. This was a young kid, maybe twenty, with a huge gash in his side that made him spill out over the highway like a deer. I could still see his hands, his sneakers. I just sat there in the car, looking.

But Andrew got moving. He found a blanket in Shan's trunk and threw it over the kid, then took his garbage bag shirt off to cover the kid's hands.

"Oh, man," the trucker said, leaning on his cab. He was shaking. I went over and sat down next to him. We just sat right down in the middle of the road.

"That's his car there," the trucker explained, pointing. "Kid was standing next to it, watching me come. I thought he was going to flag me down, but he didn't so I kept going."

The man shook his head. "But he had that look, you know?" He nodded at me, looking for understanding. "I've felt it, too. That was this kid. He was going to jump but by the time I knew it my truck was right in front of him and there he went. He was timing it."

A few weeks ago, KCRG did a piece on suicide in Iowa. Shan and I watched the story, then turned the TV off and sat in the dark. We were already in bed. I told her I knew what that feeling was like.

"Well, not exactly. I've never wanted to do it. But I've wondered. Like when I get to the top of a flight of stairs, I'll think: *I could just lean over…*"

"Really?"

"I'm not going to kill myself or anything. It's just realizing I could, you know? That there's an option."

I couldn't get it right. About how being on the edge of something can be hopeful. You realize your own power, and then you choose to come back.

"It's kind of beautiful," I said.

"Coming back isn't beautiful."

"What do you mean?"

"That's not it. What's beautiful is letting go. It's letting all this go," she waved her hands in the air. "Complete and total freedom. That's beauty."

It was her face that made me nervous. She was so calm, so sure. I asked if she wanted to talk about it, but she just smiled and kissed me goodnight. We never talked about it again.

Sitting there with the trucker, I started thinking Shan wasn't missing, that she was just where she wanted to be. But I wanted to keep believing something else: that she'd been kidnapped, or was trapped somewhere, or something else dramatic and unlikely.

Those options, terrible as they were, were better than the truth.

Andrew paced around the body, guarding it. He had a tattoo of a falling star across his left breast and one of the Morton Salt Girl on his bicep. Out in the cold wind, they both seemed a deeper blue.

That's when we heard sirens, saw the blue and red lights off in the distance.

I patted the trucker on the back and he nodded. He nodded again and again.

"I know," he said, like I'd told him something. He wiped his face with his sleeve. "I know."

Where My Father Lives Now

My father had been gone two weeks when he called up asking to see me.

"How about it, son? Come spend a night with your old man?" My father never called me *son*, and I didn't know what he meant by *old man*. My father never seemed very old to me.

"Okay," I said. I was eleven. "Where are you?"

"Put your mother on a minute. We'll get it all sorted."

I set the phone on the kitchen chair. My mother was in her bedroom, folding towels.

"Is that your father?" she asked.

I nodded. "He wants me to come visit."

"That place is for puffs." She walked past me into the kitchen and picked up the phone. "Howard?" she said. She didn't say his name happily anymore.

My father left after a spectacular fight and I hadn't seen him since. It wasn't my parents' first fight, and it wouldn't be their last, but it was the first time they threw dishes. I remember when the noise stopped, I crawled up from the basement and saw my mother standing in the middle of the kitchen with shattered dishes all around her, the air thick with dust. When she died years later from cancer, that image of her standing there, plate in hand, would come to me over and over again as I tried to sleep.

"That was your father." My mother stood in the doorway. I'd finished folding the towels and sat on the bed.

"I know," I said.

"He's at the Tomahawk downtown. You could go and stay Friday night with him, if you want. He said he'd take you to the Cattle Congress."

I'd never been to Cattle Congress. My mother always said it was for "country people." We went to Cedar Valley Days instead, the annual summer festival held in our neighborhood park. We'd walk the craft fair and sit through endless municipal band concerts and skits about our town's history. Cattle Congress was outside of town, at the fairgrounds. There were exhibition buildings filled with cows and big farm machinery, plus food, rides, and pretty girls with complicated 4-H projects. If you went to Cattle Congress, you came home dirty.

"Would you like that?" my mother asked. "You don't have to go if you don't want to."

I shrugged my shoulders. I tried not to look excited.

My mother drove me downtown that Friday. The Tomahawk was a towering, once-grand hotel whose lobby now doubled as the town bus station. A line of idling buses blocked the main hotel door, making it impossible for my mother to park. She slowed the car down and stopped beside one of the buses. A car honked behind us, but she ignored them.

"There he is. Do you see him?" All I could see were the buses and then, in between them, crowds of people walking along the sidewalk. This was my town, where I was from, but suddenly nothing was familiar.

"No."

"He's right between those first two buses. He's waving." She had me jump out and take my small suitcase from the backseat.

"And you've got Roary, right?"

"Mom," I said, embarrassed, but I was glad she asked. I quick opened the suitcase and saw his ragged paw between my pajamas. He was a small toy panther my grandfather had bought me at a circus, and I always slept with him. I would keep that ragged panther with me, from one move to the next, for my entire life.

My father came up behind me and put his hand on my shoulder.

"Hey, how are you? Good to see you, son." Again, I wondered about the *son* bit, but I let it go. It was good to see him. I put my arm around his waist and squeezed him.

"Hey hey!" he said. He rubbed my head.

"I'll get you at noon," my mother said to me. She reached over the front seat and touched my hand. "Be right here."

"Okay," I said.

"Be careful." She said this to my father.

In addition to being a bus station, the lobby was also home to a barber shop, a bakery, and, off the back, a bowling alley with a bar. I could hear the festive sound of pins crashing above all the noise in the lobby, giving the place a celebratory feeling even though the lobby was dark and smelled weird, like a mix of donuts, exhaust, and sweat. People were moving in and out, but some were making themselves at home on the ratty old furniture. Two overweight women were knitting; an old man sat in a high back chair, reading a paperback. Another man, about my father's age, was curled up on a tiny loveseat. He was sound asleep.

"Do they live here?" I asked.

My father nodded.

"Why doesn't he sleep in his room?"

"Change of scene. Don't you like to sleep on the sofa once in a while?"

The loveseat hardly looked comfortable for napping, but I didn't say anything. My father walked us over to the large, wooden staircase that led up to his room. The carpet had an elaborate swirling pattern, but was faded and worn from where people had stepped.

There was so much to take in: the enormous buffalo head that looked benevolently over the lobby; the walls cluttered with poorly framed black-and-white photographs; the strange cigarette lighter in the back corner. There was a line of payphones along one wall, and one man kept ducking in and out of the booths, searching for the one phone that kept ringing. Everything here was old and strange and somehow very adult. I loved it, all of it.

At the foot of the stairs was a wooden Indian. He towered over me and I immediately put my hand out to touch him.

"Let's see how tall you're getting." My father pressed me up against the statue. I wasn't even up to his chest.

"Someday," he said. He patted the Indian's arm.

It wasn't as great upstairs. My father's room was simple: a bed, a dresser, a worn green rug. There was a small sink and a mirror. A cot was set up in the middle of the room for me, and he put my suitcase on it.

"Where's the bathroom?" I asked.

"Down the hall. Just like at home," he smiled. "Do you need to go?"

I shook my head.

"Do you live here now?" I asked.

"For now." He went over to the sink and washed his hands. He splashed some water on his face. "It's not so bad, right? Lots of fun stuff down in the lobby."

I nodded, but seeing his shirts hanging up in the closet made me nervous. He was making himself at home somewhere else.

He untucked his shirt and dried his face on it.

"Let's just try to have a good time, okay, Tom? I've missed you."

My father went off to the bathroom. When he left the room, I took Roary out of my suitcase and held onto his paw. Then I nestled him in the bed so his head was on the pillow.

"Should we go?" my father stood in the doorway. He clapped his hands. "I bet they got the rides set up by now."

We got on a bus in the lobby that took us directly to the Cattle Congress, just dropped us off right at the gate. My father handed a man two tickets and I got my hand stamped before pushing through a turnstile.

"Would you like a map?" the man asked.

"Naw," my father said. "We'll just wander around. Right? We'll see it all."

—

Our first stop was the concourse and the dairy showmanship show. We sat on metal bleachers and I listened to my father explain what was happening: Farmers and 4-H kids had brought their animals to show. If their entry won, there was a prize involved, and the sale price of the animal went up. We watched as farmers took turns leading their animals around the track while keeping an eye on the judge.

"See that man right there? See how he keeps his hand on the heifer's shoulder? That's how he gets her to back up. He makes it look easy, but it's not easy to do."

Each time a new group would come out, the people around me would talk and cheer like they knew exactly who the contestants were, what their animals were like, and which one should win. I didn't understand what was happening, but it felt good to be part of a crowd, like we were all in this together.

"So these are their cows?" I asked.

"They're heifers," my father said. "You know what a heifer is?"

I shook my head.

"You ever hear that word before? Or steer?"

"No."

My father lit a cigarette, then blew the smoke to the side, away from me.

"You've probably never been this close to a farm animal, have you?"

I shook my head.

"Okay, now that's my fault, too," he said, putting his arm around me. He pointed to the track. "Let's catch you up. All these animals you see here are female. Now cows have had calves and heifers haven't. Calves are babies."

"Okay."

"With the males, you have steers and bulls. If you castrate a male bovine, you get a steer. You know what castration means?"

"Dad," I whispered, embarrassed.

"It's nature," he said, matter-of-fact. "Nothing to be ashamed of. You should know about nature." He rubbed his hands together. His wedding ring and class ring made a clacking sound. "What else do you want to know?"

"About heifers?"

"Anything, all right? Anything you want to know."

In that moment I wanted to ask him about Mom, about when he was coming home, but I was afraid of what he might say.

"Why doesn't Mom like Cattle Congress?"

My father stubbed out his cigarette and knocked it under the bleachers.

"Your mother's not a real curious person. This wasn't how she grew up and she doesn't take an interest. And that's fine, but it'd be nice if she wanted to come out once in a while. It's good to branch out. See another way of living."

"I like it," I said. "I like the way it smells."

"Good," he laughed. "That's good. Hey, c'mon. You want to see something else?"

After the show we got hot dogs and a can of pop—each—and made our way into every exhibition building. I read the informational signs about the different breeds of goats, looked into the large, glassy eyes of the beautiful horses. I held a baby chick and let it eat out of my hand. We didn't rush. I could ask as many questions as I wanted.

We stood in front of a pen of brightly colored ducks. A girl a little older than me sat on a folding chair beside the pen, working her way through a search-a-word book. She didn't look up.

"This is what I used to do when I was your age," my father said, leaning on the railing. "I had ducks and we'd show them every year. It's a lot of work, working with these animals. But they sure are good company."

I nodded. My father didn't talk much about his childhood. Both of his parents were dead. I'd never even been to the town where he was from.

"Your mother wouldn't care for it, but I bet you'd like a project like this."

Raising animals seemed like a very important thing to do.

"Ducks wouldn't be bad to start with." He nodded to the young girl who was still reading her book. "Would you like a duck?"

"Really?" I said. My mother would never allow a duck in the house. Not even in the backyard. There was something shifting now, I knew, but I didn't know exactly what.

"Let's see. Maybe next year. We'll see."

The other reason we never went to Cattle Congress was that it cost money. When we went to Cedar Valley Days, Mother packed sandwiches and fruit and we drank water out of the fountain. But tonight I could eat anything I wanted. Hamburgers. Fried donuts. There was no limit. The more I asked for, the more my father gave me.

"How about a chocolate malt?" he said. "Tonight we're living it up," he said to the man in the food truck, the people behind us in line. "It's boys' night out."

—

We rode The Scrambler, played the frog toss. My father managed to knock all the milk bottles over and won me a small flag that said "Cedar Rapids Cattle Congress." I would keep that flag in my locker all through high school, and on my bulletin board in college, even when the lettering had faded beyond recognition.

It was dark by the time we left. My father bought one last milk-shake, and I slurped it on the bus ride back to the hotel, covering my face with chocolate.

He put his arm around me and told other people about our adventures. Then, when the bus quieted down, I put my head on his shoulder.

"Hey kid," he kissed the top of my head. This unusual gesture made me tear up, and I blinked fast.

By the time we made it upstairs, I was starting to feel sick. I started to walk down the hall to the bathroom, then had to run to make it in time.

All of it came up, the chocolate and donuts burning my throat. Just as soon as I finished one round, I took a breath and started again.

My father kneeled down beside me and passed me Roary, like a secret. I didn't want my father to live here. I wanted him home, with me, but I knew in that instant it would never happen again. In a year my father would move to Oklahoma, and I wouldn't see him again until my high school graduation. He would come to exist only in long, beautifully written letters. I squeezed Roary's paw as I threw up again.

When I finally finished, my father peeled off my stained shirt and carried it down the hall to his room. I put my pajamas on and watched my father rinse the shirt out in his sink, rub a bar of soap over it, then rinse it again. He hung the shirt over the side of the sink to dry and it dripped on the floor, turning the carpet a dark green. The next morning I would meet my mother wearing my pajama top. I would never see that shirt again.

He came over and sat next to me on the cot. His sleeves were wet from the washing and dampened my forehead when he smoothed my hair back.

"We still had a good time tonight, though, didn't we, kid?" His voice was breaking. This was my father. "We did. We had a good time, right?"

Listen

Before Roger was a brother or a lover he was a son, and he felt this keenly when his mother called him up.

"I need an apartment," she said.

"Okay," he said. He knew his mother. "Is this a rush job?"

"I'll be there soon." He could hear her exhale, then the click of her lighter. "Just pick something out. I'm sure I'll like it."

For the last two years Roger's mother Nancy had been living on a chicken farm in Texas. Roger wasn't from Texas. Like his mother and her mother before, Roger was from Iowa— northeast Iowa— but he was the only one of his brothers and sisters still in the state. Everyone else ran out as soon as they could. Mary was in Florida. Robert was in Oklahoma. And Sam, well, Sam was in D.C. last anyone heard.

When their father died, Nancy decided she'd had enough, too.

"All you kids are gone," she'd said. "I don't see why I have to live in this old house forever. Change of scene."

She moved to Texas not knowing a soul and a few weeks later Roger got a postcard with a picture of a cowboy riding off into a sunset.

Made it fine, but it's hotter than hell. Met a woman named DeDe and I'm working on her farm, staying in my own little fixed up chicken coop. The man at the carpet store gave me all the samples so my floor's every color of the rainbow. The best stuff on the market—all for nothing. I'm moving up in the world. Hope you're moving up too. New address is here.

She didn't sign her postcards or letters. Sometimes they'd just end, or she would write "love" with a period. When Roger was younger, her letters were formal, with greetings and closings and "Mother" at the end. He thought this open ending was a testament to their friendship, to him growing up. He still signed his letters to her, but he'd reduced it over the years to "R."

Roger traveled too—west, to lands uncharted by his brothers and sisters. He moved around Arizona, from one job to the next, and every time he felt like he reached his lowest point, a letter would turn up from his mother. *After your last letter I had a feeling you might end up here,* she wrote in a letter simply addressed: *Roger Sutherland, Severa county jail (sorry I don't have any more information. Please deliver if possible).*

You can't grow anything in that desert, she wrote. *When you get out, start making your way back to Iowa.*

Roger took a few laps around his kitchen. He walked counter-clockwise. Then, when he'd exhausted one line of thinking, he started walking clockwise. Even when he pressed her, his mother still didn't say when she was coming.

"Since when are you a details man?" she said.

"I just want to make sure I can get you a place."

"You have a place, don't you?" she asked. "I'm not calling some pay phone in Cedar Rapids, am I? Cedar Rapids. I haven't seen that town since I was your age. Is there still a bar downtown called the Blue Room?"

"I have a place. You'll see it," he said.

"Good."

"I just want you to be comfortable." He could hear someone singing in the background, then a screen door slamming.

"Let's just enjoy this," she said. "Stop fussing. I've missed you."

When they hung up, he stopped pacing and called Tina.

"I need you to help me with something. If you're not busy, I mean."

"Sure," she said. "Come pick me up."

This was one of the things he liked best about Tina. She didn't ask questions. She went.

Roger had taken his mother's advice and worked his way back to Iowa, taking a job as a school janitor. He struck a friendship up with the P.E. teacher who talked Roger into joining AA, again, and sticking with it. And after some setbacks and a lot of training, Roger quit being a janitor and started working as an EMT. Things were looking up. *But it's hard, too,* he wrote his mother. *Most of my calls are for people who've been drinking and end up fighting or falling down a flight of stairs. It's not easy working on these people who just as easily could have been me.*

He met Tina a few months ago at the community center. When he was coming out of AA she was standing out in the snow, smoking, her fingers covered in some sort of acrylic paint. There was an art class that met upstairs, she explained, but now she couldn't get her car started and all her classmates were gone for the night.

It wasn't hard getting her car started, or standing around talking with her. Asking her out was the hard part. For weeks they'd run into each other and stand around and smoke, or sit at the picnic table and she'd tell him about her art. She was too young, he thought; it had been too long; he wasn't good enough. Finally she made it easy on him.

"What are you doing right now?" she said, putting out her cigarette. "I'm cold. Let's get something to eat."

Tina circled promising ads and read them out loud while Roger drove around town. The first apartment they looked at was in a small, brick building right down the hill from the college. The landlord, a skinny man with long hair, walked them to the end of the hallway, right next to a set of emergency doors.

"Go on in," Roger put his hand on Tina's back. "Tell me what you think."

When Tina walked into the apartment, Roger walked to the end of the hall and pushed out the emergency doors. They locked behind him. He tugged on them a few times, just to be sure.

"What's he doing?" the landlord asked.

"It's okay," she said. "He's thinking about emergencies. How many bedrooms?"

The windows were four feet off the ground, surrounded by neatly trimmed, very sharp bushes. He pushed his way up close and shoved each of the windows. They held. As he stood there, banging on the windows, a few people in the Jack and Jill parking lot stared at him. An employee pushing a line of shopping carts yelled. Roger waved at them and smiled.

"Windows are good," he said, walking back inside. "Grocery's next door. People pay attention around here, that's good."

The landlord looked at him strangely. Tina picked pieces of the bush off Roger's shirt.

"How much is it?" Tina asked.

"Five hundred fifty."

"For an old lady? She'll be the best tenant you have. She'll be here for years and you'll never have to worry. She'll be quiet."

"Well,"

"We've got other places to see," Tina said, turning to the door.

"Five twenty-five."

"Four seventy-five. She's on a pension."

After signing all the paperwork, they got back in the truck.

"You're something else, you know that?" Roger said.

"She could be on a pension," Tina laughed. "You on tonight?"

"Yep." He yawned as he pulled up to her place. "On call. See if I get anything."

"Well, if you get bored waiting, give me a call. I'll just be watching TV or something."

She leaned over and kissed him lightly on the mouth.

"I can be patient about this," she said, "but you got to keep talking to me. I just need to know where you're at."

"I know," he said. "I'm trying."

"I know you are." She kissed him again. "Call me later."

That night Roger stayed up and cleaned his apartment. He made his bed, laid a blanket along the couch. He cleaned out his refrigerator. The radio played old, faded country songs and he half listened to the muffled voices as he cleaned. He thought about Tina a lot, about kissing her in the car, about the conversations they had. Then he thought about the other women he'd dated, and how terrible he'd been. That person was still inside him, he knew. But there was another person too, he reminded himself, and this person was larger. This was the person scrubbing the counter.

The phone rang. He answered it.

"We got a two-car accident. Come on down."

Roger drove home the next day and found a truck idling in front of his apartment. There were two women sitting in the cab, passing a thermos back and forth. Roger parked in the driveway, then walked over. He knocked on the passenger window.

An old woman with her hair tied up in a yellow and orange scarf turned slowly, like she was expecting him.

"You Roger?" she asked, rolling down the window.

"There you are!" His mother leaned over from the driver's seat, knocking the thermos over. The other woman reached out and caught it. "We're just about ready to freeze out here. You got heat in that place?" She opened the driver's side door and gave Roger a hug.

"It's good to see you, old friend," she said, holding him. She touched his face. "There you are. Welcome back." She hugged him again. "Now," she took his arm. "Come around and meet DeDe."

When Roger got back to the truck, DeDe had already packed up her things, and his mother's things, and was ready to walk inside. She'd also neatly folded the blankets and placed them in the middle of the front seat. When Roger was a kid the family car was filled with take-out wrappers and poorly folded maps and now here was a truck with floor mats that were still in place after a twenty-hour drive.

"It's a real pleasure," DeDe said, giving him a hug. "Feel like I know you myself already."

His mother stopped to look at everything in his apartment: the banister, the pictures, the coat rack in the hall. She picked things up and hollered questions behind her. "Is this where you put your shoes?" "You still have this old thing from Aunt Liz? Let's write her. Remind me." "Can I turn on this radio? Let's get a little life in here." She was the same as she always was, but she carried herself differently. Roger watched her run from room to room. She was confident, laughing as she picked up photos and showed DeDe. She'd even lost some weight. She walked into his kitchen and spun around, admiring the tile.

While DeDe and his mother were off exploring, Roger put on a pot of tea and called Tina.

"Mom's here," he said. "She was here when I got home."

"Really?"

"She was in a truck. She's here with a friend of hers."

"Nice." He could hear her moving things around. Papers shuffling. A door opening and closing. "Can I meet her?"

"You want to?"

"Yeah. She's your mom."

He didn't say anything. He wasn't sure what to say.

"Don't think about this too much," she said. "But think about it a little. I want to meet your mom. It'd be nice." She paused. "Did she bring any chickens?"

He laughed. "No. I didn't see any."

"Well, that's disappointing."

"This is hard for me."

She sighed. "Don't say no. If you can't say yes yet, just think about it, okay? But I would like to meet her."

"Okay."

"Okay?"

"Yeah. Okay."

He hung up and saw his mother standing in the kitchen wearing one of his sweaters. "I can't believe I used to be used to all this. You mind if I borrow this? What are we eating?"

It was breakfast for dinner, something his mother used to make when they lived in Beaumont and money was tight. She'd get a dozen fresh eggs from a country friend and make pancakes and eggs. Once she cracked one in the bowl and found a beak, right there in the center of the yolk. She passed it around for the kids to see and Roger remembered it smelled awful and didn't feel anything like a beak—it was soft, almost rubbery.

"It hasn't had time to develop yet," she explained. "I cracked him too soon for that."

"Can we eat it?"

"Not this one. You can dig a hole in the backyard for this one if you want."

So he did. His mother left his sister Mary in charge of the stove and took Roger outside. He brought a spade from the garage, the one his mother used for planting tulips.

"We don't need it real deep. That's good. You want to say a little something?"

Roger shrugged. It was a wet, spring day. The rain had let up, but the whole world felt soft and he could smell the earth even before they started digging.

"Dear Lord," she began in an exaggerated voice. "We thank you for chickens with beaks, and for chickens without. We thank you for their company, for giving us dinner, and for making us laugh. We ask this in your name, amen." She tapped Roger on the head.

"Amen," he said, and laughed.

"All right, pour him in." Roger tilted the bowl and the yolk, rubbery beak and all, slid into the hole. He put his hand in the bowl and wiped out the extra bits.

"That's right. Get him all in there." He wiped his hand on the grass, then tore the grass and put it in the hole too.

"That's good. Now," she kicked the dirt back into the hole. "Let's go see about his brothers and sisters."

"Well, that's that," his mother said, putting the quiche in the oven. "You mind if we stay in your room tonight? DeDe'll never say it, but she's got a terrible back. She's older than she looks."

"Sure. I'll take you to your place in the morning."

"Has it got enough room for DeDe? We don't have much, but I'd like her to be comfortable."

"You never told me about DeDe."

"I did so. I told you all about her. Where are my letters?"

"That's not what I mean."

Nancy sat down at the kitchen table. She started putting his mail into little piles.

"Then say what you mean. I didn't raise you to not say what you mean. You didn't tell me about your girl, if you want to play that way."

Roger sighed.

"I was standing right here when you were talking. I got ears."

"I didn't know if it was anything. I don't want to hurt your feelings."

"No, no." She shook her head.

"I'm trying to be careful."

"Now," Nancy pulled out a chair and motioned for him to sit. "If there's one thing your father taught me it's that life's too short to be just hanging around on the outside being careful. For you it's different with your drinking. But you get that head of yours on straight and you go after this girl. I waited too long to be in love," she said, squeezing his hand. "Don't wait. It's worth waiting for, but don't wait if you don't have to."

That was all that was ever said about DeDe.

By the time DeDe got out of the tub they were just about ready to eat. There was the quiche, and Roger fried up some potatoes with butter and the rest of the onion. They said grace and ate quietly. Roger watched how his mother and DeDe passed things back and forth. When Nancy reached for the potatoes, she motioned to DeDe to see if she wanted any. When DeDe sliced a tomato, she gave one slice to his mother and passed her the sugar. The meal was full of small, practiced gestures.

"Well," Roger said sitting back. "You had enough?"

DeDe motioned to a deck of cards on the counter. "Nancy says you can play a few games."

"I can." Roger smiled and stacked the plates. It was good to have company, and he said so. "I'm glad you guys are here."

"You say that now," Nancy said, putting the kettle on. "Just wait until we're over all the time. I'm going to lay down a minute, that all right? I've got the kettle on for you two."

DeDe turned her head. "Take some water with you."

"I got it."

"All right. Holler if you need something."

DeDe started dealing for Rummy. She dealt quickly and the cards fell neatly into two piles. It reminded Roger of his friend Dan, who he played cards with years ago. Dan was particular about dealing, and made sure each card fell exactly on top of the last. When they weren't playing cards he and Dan worked together, drank together; they were roommates for a point. There was a time when Roger didn't go more than a few hours without talking to Dan. Now he hadn't thought about Dan in years. How did that happen?

"Your mother's health isn't good, you know." DeDe laid down a run and picked up. "She doesn't want you to know."

Roger took a minute to come back to where he was. He looked at his cards. "Why?" he said finally.

DeDe shrugged. "She's your mother. She's stubborn. I told her you're a medical man. You'd be likely to know."

"What is it?" He put down a card.

"It's her heart. She's in a bad way about it and she needs to quit smoking." She picked up another card. "Damn." She put it in her hand, then discarded the same card. "That's why we're up here. Hasn't told your family about it either, I bet."

Roger slumped back in his chair. They played a few hands in silence.

Roger picked up another card, then laid one down. He was out.

They started counting up the round.

"Does she have long?"

"I don't think it's like that." Roger started dealing and DeDe waited until she had a full hand in front of her before picking up her cards. Roger was the same way. He thought it was bad luck to pick up cards one at a time. "They didn't give her a set amount of time, but she's not going to see a hundred."

"She's only sixty-four."

"Sixty-four's still old," DeDe said, arranging her cards. "It's younger than it used to be, but it's still old."

Roger got up and brought the kettle over to the table. He took down two mugs for tea and poured.

"Are you in love with my mother?" He asked suddenly. "Sorry," he said, but he didn't mean it. He wanted to know.

DeDe looked at him and smiled. She put her cards down. "I am. And your mother is in love with me."

Roger stirred his tea. He only ever drank tea with his mother. The day she called he went out and bought a box of it. He knew they'd go through it in a week.

"It's a surprise," Roger said.

"Life'll surprise you. It surprised us, too." She picked up a card. "The Lord saw fit for Nancy to come to Texas when she did, and for us to feel the way we do. I'm not apologizing to you, and I'm not asking permission." She watched as Roger laid a card on her run, then discarded. "But it's important for me to be honest with you."

DeDe put some milk in her tea, then took a sip. "I always believed He gives you different lives inside the one you have. I think you might know something about that? How you had your life out west, now you have your life here now, and how later you'll have another life besides. It's the same for us. You just never know what to expect. You just never know where you're about to end up."

"But my mother was married."

DeDe smiled. "So was I, honey. I have children of my own."

"But how did you know?"

"How did I know I loved her?"

Roger nodded.

"Well, that doesn't change," she squeezed his hand. "That's something you know, right?"

After they finished the game, DeDe went off to bed and Roger turned to the mess in the kitchen. He took the dishes one at a time, scrubbed the counter. It was a good-looking kitchen. Clean and put away. He could hear his mother and DeDe talking in the other room, a sudden burst of laughter, then softer voices, the tired conversations before bed.

Roger made his way to the bathroom and stood before the mirror, examining his cheeks, his eyes, how his skin was hanging. His face had started clearing up and he was losing weight – not a lot, but enough to encourage him. All of this was clear right in front of him. The blurry edges of the world were starting to come into focus and it was strange and beautiful to see what he thought he'd never see again.

Tina picked up the phone on the second ring. Roger could hear laugh track from the television in the background.

"Listen," Roger said, taking a deep breath. He could hear her turning the television down. "I want to tell you something. You don't have to say anything back if you don't want to."

"Okay," Tina said.

Roger stretched the phone cord into the living room and sat down on the couch. He turned on the lamp. His hands were steady.

"Are you still there?" she said.

"Yeah," Roger said. "I'm here."

About the Author

Laura Farmer's fiction has appeared in the *Antioch Review, Camas, The Iowa Review, North American Review,* and other journals. Her novel *Catch and Release* is forthcoming from North Dakota State University Press. She directs the Dungy Writing Studio at Cornell College and is also a longtime correspondent for *The Gazette* in Cedar Rapids, Iowa.